NEVER
DANCE
WITH A
BOBCAT

Never Dance With a Bobcat

Copyright©1992,2015 by Janet Chester Bly

Published by Bly Books, P.O. Box 157, Winchester, Idaho 83555

Cover illustration: David Yorke

First printing, 1994
This printing, 2015

For a list of other books by Stephen Bly write:
Bly Books, P.O. Box 157, Winchester, ID 83555
Or check website bookstore: http://www.blybooks.com/

Dedication:
For
Paul and James Bingham
my partners
on those
south Florida
trails

CHAPTER 1

"**L**ook at that one, Nathan. Don't it look like a lady in a fancy dress dancin'?" Leah pointed to a cloud.

"It looks like a big scoop of mashed potatoes," Colin intruded. "All it needs is some gravy poured over the top."

"Colin, all you ever think about is food," she scolded.

Nathan T. Riggins tugged on a stalk of wild oats growing in the little meadow above Galena, Nevada, and began to chew. The base of the stem was still moist, and it tasted sweet as he ground it between his teeth.

"I think Colin's right. I'm hungry...reckon I'll go check on dinner."

"You boys is always hungry. Why, I'll bet it ain't 10:30 yet," Leah chided them as she wove a purple wildflower into her long brown hair.

Looking at his pocket watch, Colin countered, "It happens to be 10:48. Besides, growing boys need plenty to eat."

"Well, jist 'cause you two grew a few inches taller than me, it don't mean nothin'. Kylie Collins is taller than both of ya."

Nathan continued watching the clouds. *Oh, yeah...good old Kylie, the Perfect.*

He glanced over at the other two. "Summer's kind of boring, isn't it? You know...in a nice sort of way? Do you think Miss D'Imperio will be back next September to teach?"

"She promised," Leah replied. "I just know she'll be back."

"Are we going to go eat, or what?" Colin pressured as he began to roll up the cuffs on his long-sleeve white cotton shirt.

"Yeah. Let's see if we can find something in the pantry." Nathan stood to his feet, brushed off his gray britches, and led the others back toward town. His dog, Tona, scurried along in the sagebrush ahead of them.

"Well, I'm going to the San Francisco Millinery. Mrs. Sewell said she might have some work for me this week," Leah announced.

"You know, I need a better job," Nathan commented. "A couple hours a day at the Mercantile doesn't keep me very busy, except when a new load of freight comes in."

"Well," Colin huffed, "I just work one hour a day cleaning the bank, and I can tell you right now, that's plenty for me."

Tona let out with a warning bark. It was one of those yelps that seemed to start in his tail and build until it exploded out his mouth. Nathan realized there was some commotion in town.

"What's going on?" Colin stretched his neck to try to see around the buildings into Main Street.

"It ain't payday at the mines, and it ain't Saturday night," Leah added as the three broke into a trot.

8

Tona sprinted ahead of them and disappeared among the buildings. Nathan led the trio past the Oriental Supreme Chinese Laundry, in between Wainwright's Variety and David Isaiah's Tailor Shop, and up onto the wooden sidewalk in front of Angus McGregor's law office.

Ahead he could see a crowd gathering around a tandem freight wagon rig stretched diagonally across the street blocking traffic in both directions. The freighter with hands in the air, sat on one of his stout wheeling horses, with five teams of mules stretched out ahead of him. He was shouting at a man on the ground who waved an old Henry repeating rifle.

Nathan pushed his way through the crowd and came to a stop between a man who smelled like a saloon and a woman who smelled like spring flowers. The jerk-line still lay across the freighter's lap, but he didn't lower his hands toward the revolver in his belt. The sweat and dust of a week on the road blotched his clothing.

The man on the ground wore a dark blue shirt caked with dirt. His left boot was worn through and wrapped with a broken latigo. His hat was ripped to the crown. His red, tired eyes searched the crowd as he talked.

"Push-Bill, you ain't leaving that rig alive until I get my goods," he shouted.

"You cain't have nothin' till them wares is paid fer, and ya know it."

"My name is on the bill of ladin'. They belong to me."

"It says cash on delivery. You can read, cain't ya?"

9

The man with the gun screamed, "But I'm good for it."

"From what I hear, you couldn't buy a thirsty man a cup of water."

"When I get my goods, I'll be able to cash more ore than anyone in the state of Nevada."

The man next to Nathan shouted, "Wobley, your diggin's pinched out and you know it. Give it up."

Spinning toward the detractor, the man called Wobley fired his gun into the air above Nathan's head.

Women screamed.

The crowd scattered.

Colin froze.

Nathan pulled Leah between the freight wagons.

And Push-Bill reached down for his revolver.

Someone's going to get shot. Lord, help us!

Nathan shoved his floppy brown felt hat in front of Leah's eyes.

"What ya do that for?" she protested.

"Someone's going to get shot," he whispered.

She shoved the hat aside and peered around the wagon. "Here comes your daddy."

Marshal Riggins, standing taller than Nathan had ever seen him, marched in between the two gun-waving men.

"Wobley, give me that rifle!" He stretched out his left hand, his right hand remaining on the polished oak grip of his still holstered revolver.

"Marshal, this man won't give me my goods. So don't press me. I swear I'll shoot you and him both."

"You're not shooting anybody today," Marshal Riggins replied.

"Your daddy is wearin' them shootin' eyes," Leah whispered.

"What?" Nathan murmured.

"Miss Patsy told me you can tell if a man is goin' to shoot by lookin' at his eyes. Your daddy's sportin' shootin' eyes, and them fellas know it."

Without taking his focus off Wobley, the marshal called out, "Push-Bill, you holster that gun, slide down off that wheel horse, and go inside the Mercantile. Do you hear me?"

Lifting himself off the horse, the freighter groused, "He don't get them goods, do you hear, Marshal? He don't get them until—"

"Push-Bill, get inside," the marshal thundered.

"Yes, sir...I'm goin'...don't let that weasel shoot me in the back, Marshal."

Ignoring the freighter, the marshal looked straight at Wobley. "Give me the Henry."

"Nope, I won't. I got to have them supplies. Don't ya see? If I don't get 'em, I'm busted. I'll shoot ya, I swear, Marshal. That diggin' is all I got in this world. I ain't goin' to lose it now."

"Wobley, give me the rifle," Marshal Riggins repeated.

Nathan strained to see his father's eyes.

Leah's right. Daddy won't back down now. Lord, help him. There's nothing in those wagons worth getting anyone shot...especially Daddy.

"Marshal, you don't understand," the man pleaded.

"Wobley, look around you. There isn't a man on this street that hasn't gone belly-up in the mines

11

once or twice. I lost every penny I had to my name at Willow Creek. Pull yourself up and go on."

"Yeah, that's easy for a man with a job, a fine wife, and a family to say. I ain't got nothin'...nothin'! Do ya hear me?"

"Wobley, I'll tell you what you have. You have two choices. Either you're going to die right here on this dirty street in a dusty, little, no-account Nevada town...or you can hand me that rifle. Now if you give me that gun, I'll see that you get a bath, a shave, and a hot dinner at the New Orleans Hotel. Then you can leave town and find yourself something better. It's your turn. Choose."

"It ain't fair," Wobley hollered. "If I'd a had them supplies six months ago, I'd be the one living up on the hill in that big house."

"Wobley, give me the gun, or I'm going to shoot you. But I'm not planning on missing dinner 'cause of you."

"Do I get my gun back when I leave town?"
"Yep."
"You goin' to throw me in the hoosegow?"
"Nope."

Wobley took a big deep breath and sighed.

"There ain't goin' to be no shootin'," Leah whispered, putting one hand on Nathan's shoulder and pointing with the other. "Look at your daddy now."

Nathan could see the tense lines relax. He had seen it before hundreds of times.

Leah's got it straight. It's all over.

"Marshal, kin I order one of them black Louisiana steaks?" Nathan's dad cracked a generous smile. "Wobley, you can order a double helping of okra if you want. Now hand me that gun."

"You can have the gun," Wobley said with a nod, "but I ain't eatin' no slimy okra. I'd just as soon take lead."

The marshal seized the man's gun, and people streamed out

from hiding places and milled in the streets. The hushed conversations soon burst into a roar.

"You goin' to lock him up, Marshal?" someone shouted. "Nope. He's got a good-bye meal coming. But he doesn't get it 'til he takes a bath. Now you folks go on and do something constructive instead of standing and staring. Nate, come over here."

"Yes, sir."

"You go into the Mercantile and tell Push-Bill to get out here and park these wagons someplace else. Then head on home and tell your mother I'll be taking dinner at the New Orleans Hotel."

"Yes, sir. I will." Nathan sensed someone standing behind him.

"Miss Leah," the marshal nodded at her, "you're looking mighty fine today. Those flowers look right handsome in your hair."

"Thank ya, Marshal. It's a pity your son didn't inherit your keen eyesight." She wrinkled her nose at Nathan and then continued, "That sure was a brave thing you did—backing down Mr. Wobley like that."

"He's not bad. It just hits a man hard when he's worked so strenuous and lost everything."

Nathan banged his boots into the worn wooden sidewalk as he scurried into the Mercantile shouting, "Push-Bill, it's all over. Daddy says to move that team out of the road."

"Thanks, son. Your daddy's a good man."
Push-Bill rubbed his chin and peeked out the front
door. Finally, the freighter ventured out onto the
sidewalk.

"Say, son...you want to make a few dollars
this afternoon?"

"Yes, sir," Nathan shouted.

"Well, after dinner come on around to the
back of the Mercantile. I'll hire ya to help unload
these wagons."

"I'll be there."

Nathan scrambled over to Leah waiting
outside and escorted her toward her house. She
grabbed Nathan's arm and skipped across the
dusty street.

"I betcha when you get older, you'll be brave
like your daddy," she declared.

"I hope so, but I'm not too sure," Nathan
admitted.

"How come you didn't want me to watch?"
she asked. "'Cause there are some things a woman
shouldn't have to see."

"You sayin' I'm a woman?" she teased.

Nathan caught himself looking carefully at
Leah. "You know what I meant." He felt his cheeks
turn hot.

"Well, next time why don't you ask me before
you go shovin' an old sweaty hat in my face?"

"I do have something to ask you." Nathan
grinned.

"Oh yeah? What's that?"

"Well, you said a person could tell whether
another was about to shoot by looking at his eyes."

"Yep. That's what Miss Patsy told me."

"Well," Nathan quizzed, "how did you get so chummy with Miss Patsy? My daddy says if he ever catches me over on Murphy Street, he'll tan me so hard I'll have to sleep standing up."

"Well, Miss Patsy don't spend all her time over on Murphy Street. I help with the fittin' on her dresses. She says when I get more...you know, more mature, she'll give me some of her old ones. So there!" She dropped Nathan's arm and ran up the stairs of the house without looking back.

◆ ◆ ◆ ◆ ◆

Nathan spent little time scraping down a plate of hot beef stew, a fist-sized chunk of bread, and a very large helping of peach cobbler. He quickly carried his dishes to the kitchen counter, waved at his mother, and rushed out the door. Finding Push-Bill Horn rolling back the canvas tarps on his wagons, Nathan climbed up on the front one and began to help. Most of the products were in wooden crates, but Nathan enjoyed reading about the contents just the same.

The entire front wagon was full of mining gear. There were gauges, fittings, pulleys, reducing screens, bolts, and big odd-shaped boxes bearing the printed warning, "Do Not Open! For Shiloh Mining Company only!"

It took over an hour for the two of them to unload the wagon. Nathan's arms pained as they turned toward the second one. In it he found bolts of cloth for Mr. Isaiah, ready-mix paint for Central Nevada Sign Painting, a box of buckles for the livery, a crate of dishes packed in sawdust for the New Orleans Hotel, four one-hundred-pound sacks of sugar for the Deluxe Bakery, a rattling crate for the Modern Stationers...among other unidentified boxes.

When both wagons were empty, Nathan plopped down on the tailgate of the back wagon, panting.

"You a little tired, son?" Push-Bill asked.

"Yeah...I don't...you know...do that much lifting most the time."

"You still going to school, ain't ya?"

Nathan jumped down from the wagon and walked up to Push-Bill. "Yeah...I mean, no. I'm going to school, but we don't have class again until September."

"September, huh?" Push-Bill yanked himself back up on his wheeling horse. "Well, listen. I need a helper during the summer. I'm plannin' on haulin' freight all summer up to 10. I'll need a lad like yourself to grease axles and to wrangle the mules. It will be nine days out, then three days back here in town. After that we'll start all over again. You got a horse?"

"Yes, sir."

"Is he sound?"

"Yes, sir."

"Good. Well, if you supply a horse and bedroll, I furnish the grub and a fresh bed at 10. And I'll pay you $9 cash every trip."

"You will?" Nathan gulped.

"Yep."

"Push-Bill..Nathan paused. "Eh...what's this 10? You said you're freighting to 10. Ten what?"

"10. That's the town. 10, Nevada. It's up there near the Owyhee. Ain't you heard about that strike?"

"The town's name is just 10?"

"Yep. I guess them old boys got tired of inventing names, only to have the town go bust anyway. So this one they just call 10. Do you want the job?"

"When are you going to roll out?" Nathan asked.

"In three days."

"I'll have to ask my parents, but if they let me, I'd like the job." Push-Bill picked up the jerk-line and slapped it against the teams. "Say, can you shoot a gun?" he called back.

"Yes, sir. I shoot a carbine pretty fair," Nathan hollered. Then he thought to call out, "Why?"

The creak of the wagon wheels drowned out the teamster's reply.

◆ ◆ ◆ ◆ ◆

Late that night, with Nathan tucked underneath a single flannel sheet, he heard his mother and father debating whether or not to allow him to accept the job. He could tell they disagreed. Most of the night, Nathan didn't agree with himself either.

I really, really want the job...but I'm scared. I mean, it's hard work...and kind of dangerous, I think. And I'd miss Mom and Dad and Colin and Tona.

Maybe I can take Tona with us.

And I'd miss Leah.

Really? Is that true? The part about missing Leah? Lord, it's kind of confusing.

17

◆ ◆ ◆ ◆ ◆

By breakfast the next morning, four factors convinced Nathan to accept the summer job.

First, his father said it would be a good way for him to build up some strength and learn a little about freighting.

Then his mother said he could go, but he had to promise to read his Bible, keep his hands and face clean, and eat some fruit and vegetables every day.

And Push-Bill Horn, whom he saw at the corrals when he went to feed his horse, Onepenny, told him he could bring Tona as long as the dog didn't cause them any bother.

But the last and deciding factor tumbled into place when he ran into Leah at the post office.

"Nathan, look here. Guess who I got a letter from?"

"Ulysses S. Grant?"

Leah stuck out her tongue and danced around on the wooden sidewalk. "No, it's from Kylie. Kylie Collins."

"You mean the one who never shows up on the stage?" he teased.

"I mean the one I ain't never goin' to marry anyone else but him."

"Is he promising to come see you again?"

"He's coming," she announced, "sometime this summer."

"Tell him hello. I'll be gone," Nathan informed her.

"You goin' away the whole summer?"

"Yep."

"You ain't either," Leah fumed. "You're jist jealous."

After a heated seven-minute explanation, Leah was in tears. "Nathan, you cain't go now. Kylie is really coming to see me. You got to be here. It's very important," she sobbed, brushing away tears with the back of her hand.

"Leah, if it's all that important, I'll...I'll make sure I visit with him when I'm back in town. It will only be nine days. I really don't understand the—"

"You don't understand nothin', Nathan T. Riggins." She turned on her heels and stomped back toward her father's barbershop. While Nathan stared in puzzlement, Leah turned around and sneered. "And you can tell your mother I ain't cornin' to no party neither."

"What? Party? What party?" Nathan choked.

Leah cried out, "Oh, no, I didn't say nothin'." Then she hauled up her dress above her ankles and ran home.

"Nice work, Riggins. You certainly charmed her this morning."

Nathan turned to see Colin walking up.

"Party?" Nathan mumbled.

"What did you say?" Colin asked.

"What's this about a party?"

Colin shrugged. "Hey, it wasn't my idea. I told them there was no way of keeping it a secret. 'He'll find out, so why not just make it public?' Oh, no. No one would listen. It was your mother and Leah that dreamed it all up."

"Dreamed up what?" Nathan pressed.

"The surprise birthday party, of course...my word, wasn't that what we were talking about?" Colin gasped.

19

"Tomorrow's my birthday."

"Everyone in town knows that," Colin assured him.

"I didn't know," he confided.

"Well, there you go. Now you do. We don't have to go around whispering anymore."

"I think I might have hurt Leah's feelings. Maybe I'd better go talk to her."

"Why the big rush? You've got all summer," Colin insisted.

"That's the problem." Nathan sighed. "I've only got three days."

CHAPTER 2

On Tuesday, June 22, 1878, Nathan T. Riggins had his almost-surprise thirteenth birthday party.

His father presented him a hand-tooled scabbard for his carbine and a box of scatter shells for "shooting snakes."

His mother handed him a copy of *The Adventures of Tom Sawyer* and four pairs of socks.

Colin gave him a full pound of St. Louis creme-filled chocolates and then proceeded to eat half of them himself.

Leah surprised him with a rich green shirt that she had made. "I ain't too good at it yet, but I think that color will look awful princely on ya," she said blushing.

It seemed to Nathan that every kid in Galena was there at his party. They laughed, ate, ran, played, ate, sang, opened presents, and ate again.

The sun had just dropped behind the western hills when the party ended and Nathan walked Leah home. They sat down on a faded wooden bench in front of her father's barbershop.

"That was a good party, Nathan...even if I almost ruined it." Leah sighed.

"It sure was. I really like my new shirt. I'm impressed."

21

"You know, I'm making myself a dress out of that material. Maybe sometime we could wear them at the same time."

"Sure. How about when I come back home in nine days?"

"Kylie might be here," she reminded him.

"I know. That's why I want to wear it."

Leah wrinkled her nose and exclaimed, "You going to try to make him jealous?"

"Isn't that why you wanted me to be here when he arrived?" She lowered her head. "Yeah...I guess."

"You know what, Leah...I think that party was kind of sad, too."

"Sad? Why you ain't that old, Nathan."

"You know how we ran around and played games and laughed at each other? Well, how many more birthdays do you think we'll act that way?"

"Everything's changin', ain't it?"

He glanced at her eyes and nodded. "Yeah, sort of like we're supposed to be grown up—"

"But we ain't yet," she interrupted.

"I'm not sure I want to quit being a kid."

"You know, Nathan, before you moved to town last year, I hated being a kid."

"Really?"

"All I could think about was getting old enough to get married and move out on my own. But this last year...I especially liked this year. You made it fun 'cause you always treat me nice. I mean, most of the time you treat me nice. And you bought me them shoes, and you never teased me about the way I talk or that I don't read very good."

"Well, I'll have to admit, Leah, it's been about the best year of my life. I learned a whole lot about the West and about Indians and horses and gold mining and buffaloes and stuff. I learned to trust God more, and I sure learned that He gives me special friends like Leah Walker."

She reached over and put her hand on top of Nathan's as it rested on the bench between them. He turned his hand over and gripped hers.

"Can I really wear that new shirt in front of Kylie?"

"Yep."

"What if he gets jealous?"

"He'd be the first boy who ever got jealous over me." She feigned a pout.

"No, seriously...what if he's really jealous?"

"Then he'll beat you up." Leah shrugged.

"That's a fact I reckon I'll have to ponder."

Nathan stood and released her hand. "I guess I better get back home and pack a few things. We're leavin' at daybreak, you know."

"I see you in nine days then?"

"Yep."

"Good-bye, Nathan. Say a prayer when you think about me."

"Sure." He walked about five steps and then turned. "Leah?"

"Yeah?"

"It felt good, didn't it?"

"What?"

He hesitated. "You know...holding hands."

"Yeah, it did." Then she straightened up and teased, "Now go on home...cowboy!"

He could see her watch him through the twilight shadows as he disappeared down the

23

street. But he could almost hear her mumble in a monotone under her breath, "But I ain't never goin' to marry nobody but Kylie Collins."

And if he could see through the Nevada dusk, he'd have spotted the tears that traced paths down her cheeks.

◆ ◆ ◆ ◆ ◆

Promptly at 6:00 a.m. on Wednesday morning, two tandem wagons pulled by one team of stout wheel horses and five teams of mules rolled out of Galena headed for the upper reaches of the Independence Mountains and the mining town of 10, Nevada.

Faded red wheel spokes, dust-caked blue boxes, the name "J. Murphy" almost worn away. Only the bleached canvas tops looked new. A matched pair of white mules pulled in the lead, and the big horses were teamed next to the front wagon. Push-Bill Horn sat astride the left wheeler whom he called Rosie.

Tona alternated between leading the procession and following the spotted horse. Nathan rode Onepenny alongside Push-Bill. He waved good-bye to his dad and searched the street to see if Leah had come to see him off.

She hadn't.

It took Nathan only about thirty minutes to realize that freighting was a very slow business.

"What's the schedule, Push-Bill? How far do we travel today?"

"Today 17.5 miles, 15.2 tomorrow, 12.6 the next, 14.5 the following, and 5.4 tough miles up Wild Horse Canyon. That puts us into 10 by

Saturday noon...providin' we don't have troubles with outlaws, Indians, flash floods, broken axles, snakes, or women folk," he roared.

By the time they reached camp that night, Nathan figured it had been the longest day in the history of the world. Just one plodding step after another.

One hour. Stop to let the animals relieve themselves.

Two more hours. A thirty-minute break to let them out to eat.

Another two hours. It's dinner time. Unhitch the whole team and let them graze.

By 1:30 p.m. back on the trail until a half-hour break two hours later. Two more hours and camp for the night.

Lord, I guess this is how real work is supposed to be.

Nathan's job had been mostly greasing the hubs, scouting ahead for Push-Bill, and tending mules during the breaks. He was amazed at how the freighter seemed to know exactly the mood of each animal and how to coax the best out of it.

But it was around the fire as they ate their supper, after tying the horses and mules to a picket line, that he learned the most.

"Now, Nate, don't you ever picket Whitey and Snowflake next to the other mules. They don't get along with them. Seems they consider it below their dignity to associate with an ordinary swing mule. That's why I always put Rosie and Roanie in between them. Those two hosses seem to git along with all their cousins.

"Ya see, being in the lead tends to spoil an animal quick. They don't never want to go back to

25

the line. Can't say that I blame them though. Up there in the lead you get to gaze across some mighty winsome country. But the rest that's stuck in the pack...well, all they ever get to see is the rear end of the animal ahead. And that ain't much of a view even for a mule.

"You done a good job today, Nate. I appreciate the help. It gets a might lonely out here hauling freight by yourself. In the old days, a man wouldn't set out unless he had a dozen teamsters pullin' with him. But things is changed. It's more settled now, at least until we git to 10."

"Do we have a place like this to camp every night?" Nathan asked.

"Nope. Tomorrow we'll make it to Bobcat Springs, which is as purdy a place as you'll find in Nevada. Then we have a couple of meager nights in the mountains, especially Friday night in Wild Horse Canyon. But by Saturday night we'll be at the Colorado House, eatin' steaks and drinkin' ..." Push-Bill looked over at Nathan. "Eh...drinkin' coffee, yes, sir."

Nathan stared across the campfire and up at the quickly darkening sky. He could already see the twinkle of several stars. "Push- Bill? Do we sleep under the wagons or by the mules?"

"Both. You take the wagon, and I'll guard the mules. But you sleep with that carbine handy."

"You think there will be trouble tonight?"

"Yep."

"What makes you say that?" Nathan asked.

"'Cause ever' time I decide that there ain't no trouble, it comes an' looks me up for sure. So I figure on trouble ever' night...and, by golly, it don't ever come."

"So what is the trouble we're planning for—that won't come? Indians?"

"Probably not. We jist got to watch out and try and keep the animals from gettin' spooked or scattered. I'll go settle them down. You can turn in if you want to."

"I promised my mom I'd do some readin'," Nathan informed him.

"Well, never disappoint your mama, son. Even old teamsters know that."

As Push-Bill Horn was walking toward the animals, Nathan called out, "What time are we getting up?"

"I'll roust you out. 'Course if we was camped by Echo Canyon, it would be different."

Nathan dug in his bedroll for his Bible.

"What's Echo Canyon?" he asked.

Push-Bill Horn sauntered back by the fire and squatted down. He picked up a small stick and began to scratch on the ground.

"Well, son...you've no doubt been next to a canyon wall a time or two where you had an echo. You shout 'hello there!' and pretty soon those words bounce right back at you."

"Sure," Nathan said with a nod, "like up on Lewis Mountain."

"Yeah, that's the drift. But Echo Canyon is up on the Yellowstone. It's so deep and wide that the echoes are almost like magic. Why, one night me and Old Jim Bridger were up there—"

"You know Jim Bridger?" Nathan gasped.

"Bridger, Carson, Fremont—I know'd 'em all. But as I was sayin'...me and Old Jim was up on the Yellowstone, camped right on the rim of Echo Canyon. Now you ain't never seen a canyon like it,

27

exceptin' you was in Arizona. And this one on the Yellowstone is an echo canyon too. So I was all tucked into my roll nice and smooth when Old Jim started hollerin' at the top of his voice down into the canyon."

"What did he yell?" Nathan asked.

"He screamed, 'Push-Bill, get out of bed, you lazy bum, it's morning.'"

Nathan pulled off his hat and ran his fingers through his hair. "I thought you said it was evening."

"It was. That's why it was so strange. Well, Old Jim comes shuffling back to the fire and crawls under his blankets without explaining nothin'. Naturally, I don't insult him by asking questions. Well, son, I was sound asleep dreaming of wild horses or something jist before daybreak, and all of a sudden this eerie voice comes rolling out of the canyon.

"What did it say?" Nathan pressed.

"'Push-Bill, get out of bed, you lazy bum, it's morning!' That's when I woke up, and, sure enough, Bridger was sittin' at the fire boilin' coffee. He said there's an eight-hour delay on that echo if you know'd how to do it."

Nathan stared up at Push-Bill who was sporting a five-day beard. A smile broke across the freighter's face.

"Nate, don't you go believin' one word from a teamster's mouth when he's sittin' around the fire at night. We ain't got nothin' to do but pull a few stretchers."

After Push-Bill went to bed, Nathan read the first chapter of the book of Matthew, then put up his Bible, slipped off his boots, and climbed into the bedroll under the lead wagon. Tona slept only a few feet away.

He thought about cool breezes, bright stars, wagons that creaked slowly, and Leah Walker. He figured he was tired and would probably fall asleep quickly.

He was right.

Nathan didn't really feel wide awake until the first stop the next morning about two and a half miles from their evening camp. After that he was back in the grueling routine...riding...walking...greasing the hubs...tending mules...and plenty of sweat. The insides of his knees rubbed raw on the ducking britches, his right arm cramped, and his back ached whenever he slouched in the saddle. No wonder cowboys are always 'sittin' tall.'

By the time they rolled into Bobcat Springs, he knew it would be a long dusty summer, and he figured he would have honestly earned every penny he made. After supper Nathan lay on the ground with his bedroll as a pillow under the small part of his back. The smell of fried meat still lingered in the cooling night air. The conversation turned to bobcats.

"I been coming though this canyon for eighteen months," Push-Bill announced, "and I only seen one bobcat in here. 'Course that's 'bout what should be expected."

"How come?" Nathan had his pocket knife out and was trying to cut a matted fur ball off Tona's back side.

"Them bobs is mighty quick fellas. They're 'bout as sneaky as a Texas outlaw as far as keepin' out of sight. Then they don't run in packs neither.

Always alone. Oh, a mama might have her cubs for a while, but when it's time to kick 'em out, they're all on their own.

"Now I want to tell ya, them is mean animals. Don't you ever dance with a bobcat. Do ya savvy? If they want to run, let 'em run, but don't pin 'em down. They'll jump ya. And they never lose a fight."

"Never?" Nathan pressed.

"Nope. They'll fight ya until they win or die...but they won't slink away a loser."

"How big are they, Push-Bill? They aren't as big as Tona, are they?"

"Nope. Now a cougar can grow that size, but a bobcat is about half the size of your dog."

Nathan pulled off his right boot and rubbed his toes. "What do they eat out here?"

"Rabbits, mainly, I suppose. Rodents, birds...maybe a baby deer or antelope. I ain't never seen it myself."

Sitting up, Nathan jammed his boot back on his foot. "When's the best time to spot one?"

"There ain't no good time," Push-Bill lectured. "But I suppose right before daylight if you scanned the water's edge, you just might catch sight of one coming in for a drink."

"Push-Bill, how do I know you're not just telling windies like you did last night?"

The teamster pushed back his dirty hat and grinned from ear to ear. "Ya don't, son...ya don't."

◆ ◆ ◆ ◆ ◆

It was still dark when Nathan felt a boot in the side, nudging him awake.

30

"Nate...if you want to have a chance at seeing a bobcat, you'd better slip on down to the water nice and quiet."

Nathan bolted straight up. "Did you see one?"

"I didn't look," Push-Bill replied, "but it will be your only chance this trip."

Nathan considered it fortunate that Tona had wandered off into the brush somewhere. He figured with his dog along, he would never get close enough to see a bobcat. At this time of the year the springs were no more than a small pond surrounded by grass, with a few bushes tucked on the south side. After sloshing through the mud, Nathan squatted in the brush and waited for more daylight.

He waited.

And waited.

And waited some more.

His legs began to cramp, and some kind of small, but fierce flying bug was feasting on the back of his neck.

What am I doing here? Is Push-Bill playing a trick on me? Maybe this is all a joke. He said that I shouldn't believe anything he said around the campfire at night. He played me for a sucker. It's like going on a snipe hunt. It's just a game for greenhorns.

Nathan had resigned himself to going back to camp to face Push-Bill Horn's laughter, when sudden movement along the water's edge caught his eye. His nerves jumped tight, then relaxed as the supposed bobcat turned out to be a rabbit eating the green grass on the water's edge.

31

I wonder what a bobcat looks like. Well, they must have a bobbed-off tail. And resemble a cat.

Suddenly a reddish-brown spotted blur flashed in front of his eyes, pounced on the rabbit, and, with a savage flip, broke its victim's neck. For a split second the animal hovered over the dead rabbit and glared at Nathan. A cold chill hit him as he glimpsed the animal's yellow-green eyes.

Bobcat!

Instantly, the animal and its breakfast disappeared into the brush.

Nathan gulped a big deep breath.

It was *a bobcat!*

"Push-Bill," he shouted as he ran back for the wagons. "Push- Bill, I saw one. There was a bobcat down there. I really saw one. It wasn't a stretcher, was it?"

The freighter glanced up from his nearly boiling cup of coffee and grinned.

"'Course it ain't no stretcher. This is Bobcat Springs. What did he look like?"

"Well, he was about twice the size of a big house cat and reddish-brown, mostly brown, with a white-looking belly and dark brown streaks and spots, sort of like a leopard...and a short tail, maybe four to six inches, and a broad face...and strong—he looked like a regular cat with muscles." Nathan paused long enough to catch his breath. "And he had yellow-green eyes."

"You got that close, did ya?" Push-Bill asked.

"Yeah, I was in the bushes not more than twenty feet away."

"Don't ever plan on gettin' closer unless you have your gun pointed and you consider yourself a good shot. Bobcats will fight anything, anytime.

They don't get along with nothin' on this earth except themselves. Sort of like freighters I guess." He smiled.

Nathan bristled with excitement as he stirred up the fire and piled some beans on his tin plate. He could instantly taste the fire of Push-Bill's "Loredo Juice" seasoning.

"So now you've seen a bobcat," the old freighter mused, ignoring Nathan's gasping for cold air on his scorched tongue. "I'll tell ya somethin', and this ain't no stretcher neither. There ain't one man in a thousand who's ever seen one that close, no sir."

"It was kind of scary," Nathan admitted, grabbing for his canteen. "I mean, it's just a little animal, but his eyes looked...well, they sort of reminded me of my dad's eyes the other day when he thought he was going to have to shoot Wobley."

"How's that?"

"Determined to fight and win," Nathan replied. "That bobcat took one look at me and was determined to fight and win."

"Yep, I reckon he did."

Nathan's eyes watered as he finished his breakfast and rinsed off his plate with some boiling coffee. "Push-Bill, where are we headed today?"

"Well, we'll swing near the Rialto ranch and then start the climb up Wild Horse grade."

"The Rialto ranch?"

"Yep. Don't seem possible that anyone would try to make it up in this remote place, does it? Hope them girls is o.k."

"Girls?" Nathan quizzed.

33

"Yep...I hear the mama and daddy died a few years back, and their seven girls is trying to keep the place going all by themselves."

"Seven girls? How old are they?" Nathan pressed.

"I ain't rightly sure, but it's a fact there'll be a passel about your size. But don't let your tongue loll out. We ain't goin' back in there."

"Why not?"

"'Cause the road's bad, and I hear they have a tendency to shoot at anyone who comes up the driveway. They is a cautious bunch any way you cut it, if you get the drift."

CHAPTER 3

At the first stop out of Bobcat Springs to rest the animals, Nathan caught sight of what looked like trees at the base of a barren mountain range on the western horizon. Other than the blue sky, they offered the only color in the sand- brown landscape of the northern basin.

"What's over there?" He pointed.

"That's the Rialto ranch."

Nathan's eyes shot back and forth. "You mean all those girls you told me about?"

"Yep. Providin' they haven't starved, got carried off by Indians, or died of pneumonia."

"Maybe we ought to go check on them," Nathan suggested.

Push-Bill stared him right in the eyes and then snorted, "Wagh!"

"What I mean is," Nathan hurried to explain, "somebody ought to check on them." He looked away.

"I know exactly what you mean. I ain't that old," Push-Bill roared. "One of these days...on the return trip maybe we'll mosey off that way. But the quicker I get these goods to 10, the more money I make. That boom will last till Christmas at best. After that, everyone will be broke or consolidated."

"Consolidated?"

35

"Right now there's a thousand little claims, none of them big enough to run a full-scale operation. So some San Francisco company of bankers and lawyers will come in and buy them all out and put in one or two mines, open some company stores, and put us all out of business."

Nathan swung his left leg over the saddle horn and now sat sideways facing Push-Bill as the freighter remounted Rosie. "How big a place is 10?"

"Anywhere from 200 to 2,000." Push-Bill gazed at the horizon. "Look up there...here comes a pilgrim from that direction now."

Nathan eyed a man walking down the road. He carried a small pack on his back and a four-foot walking stick in his right hand. His felt hat had the entire top ripped off, and his jacket was patched, his boots worn clear through so that several toes showed. His scraggly beard showed flecks of gray.

"Ho! On the wagon. May I have a word with you before you roll on?"

"Pull out your carbine and watch the horizon, Nate," Push- Bill cautioned.

"He doesn't look dangerous."

"Nope, but he might be a setup for others. You keep a lookout, and I'll deal with this old boy."

Nathan laid his carbine across his lap and kept it pointed in the direction from which the man had appeared. The steel trigger guard felt hot to his touch.

"I say," the man shouted, "this is as fortunate for me as it is for you, my friends."

"How's that?" Push-Bill growled.

"Well, excuse me, Colonel, but I have something I would like to show you. You are headed to 10, aren't you?"

36

"What if I am?"

"Now...we just might be able to help each other out. You see, I've spent the past several weeks in the town and have purchased interest in several mining claims. But now—"

Push-Bill spat a wad of tobacco juice into the dirt between them and wiped his mouth on his sleeve. "And you want to sell them to me for some inflated price?"

"No, sir...I would never try to pull that on anyone, especially one as knowledgeable as yourself. I would like to sell them at an extremely modest price. You see, I lost my horse back up the road a spell and have need to reach Battle Mountain Station to talk to my bankers. But I will need a horse and supplies to reach the railroad."

He reached into his coat pocket and pulled out a wad of papers. "You see, I've got a few feet in the Lucky Seven Mine, some in the Alligator, the Pretty Nugget, the Root-Hog-Or-Die, the Pennsylvania Dutch, the Broken Nose, the Cedarwood, twenty-five feet in the All-Is-Lost (now that's a fine piece) and—"

"So you're going to make me a good deal by letting me buy the works for a surprising low amount."

"Yes, sir, I am. Just cause I'm in a bind, and I could let go a few of these admittedly small parcels, but I assure you they are rich ones. I'll sell, say, eight of them to you and your son for...$20 cash and a horse."

"Mister, I was in Califomy in '49. After that there was Kern River, Fraser River up in the British possessions, then the Comstock. I've been from Florence to Prescott hauling goods. I've heard every spiel known to man and a few made up by the devil himself. I didn't buy claims then, and I'm not buying any now." Push-Bill cracked the jerk-line and the wagons began to roll.

"Son...forget the cash." The man turned toward Nathan. "I'll just trade you straight across— these valuable claims I mentioned for that spotted pony of yours."

"Mister," Nathan replied, "I wouldn't trade this horse for every claim on Mt. Davidson." He spurred Onepenny ahead, then reined up, and spun him back to the man on foot.

"I'll give you a dozen strips of beef jerky for those claims," he called out.

"You drive a hard bargain, son...but it's a deal."

Nathan reached into his saddlebag and pulled out the jerky, which was wrapped in a worn linen cloth. The bundle felt greasy in his hand, and he could smell the aroma of peppered meat. The man handed the tattered papers up to Nathan and reached out to shake his hand.

"What's your name, son?"

"Nathan T. Riggins."

"Well, Nathan T. Riggins, they call me Washoe Willy. Sure hope them claims bring you better luck than they brought me. Where's the next watering hole?"

"Two and a half miles straight ahead. It's called Bobcat Springs."

Nathan watched Washoe Willy trudge on down the road. Then he turned Onepenny toward the dust cloud of the wagons and galloped up to Push-Bill's side.

"Did you buy them claims?" Push-Bill asked.

"Yeah."

"What did you give him?"

"Twelve pieces of beef jerky."

"You got suckered, boy."

"They probably aren't real, are they?"

"Maybe. Maybe not. But even if they're real claims, they're claims to an empty hole."

Nathan looked through the papers. "This one—the twenty- five feet of the All-Is-Lost—is drawn up and signed by some California lawyer. It looks official."

"California lawyer? That's the most worthless of them all. Ain't good for nothin' but startin' a fire."

Nathan tucked the papers into his saddlebag. "Well, I'll just keep them anyway...sort of a souvenir."

"Well, I'm glad you got it out of your system. When we get to 10, there'll be a man on every street corner selling claims, and I don't want you to be an embarrassment."

"They have street corners in 10?" Nathan quizzed.

A loud roar boiled up from Push-Bill Horn. "Hah! Those streets, or what you might call streets, is so crooked there ain't a corner in the whole town. No sidewalks. No city parks. And no law. You'll see when we get there."

"When will that be?"

"Good Lord willin', it'll be noon Saturday."

◆ ◆ ◆ ◆ ◆

It was closer to 3:00 P.M., Saturday, June 26, 1878, when Nathan first caught sight of 10,

Nevada. All morning long lines of traffic going into town had increased. Horses, wagons, and stagecoaches rolled past them. And Push-Bill lived up to his name, shouting his team past several oxen-pulled freight wagons.

Nathan marveled at the height and steepness of the terrain they now climbed. Treeless, the naked peaks of the mountains huddled under a streaked powdering of leftover winter snow. Halfway up the side of the steepest one clung the town of 10, like a barnacle to a ship's hull.

Nathan stared in amazement. How could anyone build on something so steep? The back of every building perched on stilts, and many builders hadn't bothered to make them level. Nathan figured that over half the buildings were canvas-topped, and tents were scattered anywhere there was ten feet of flat space.

The crowd got thicker as they approached the city. By the time they reached the first building, what street there was left was so filled with people that Push-Bill had to pull to the side and stop.

"Nate," he shouted. "You watch this rig. I'm going to see who's buyin'."

Nathan tied Onepenny to the wagon and climbed up on Rosie, taking the teamster's position. From that height he studied the people who crammed 10. The crowd was mostly male, mostly bearded, and mostly scroungy. Many looked like typical miners and prospectors—here to dig ore, hoping to strike color. The rest seemed intent on peddling something to the others—everything from mining gear to meals, from frying pans to gold pans, from baked goods to alcohol. Off to one side he saw several men waving slips of paper, haggling and shouting insults.

He face lit up when Push-Bill Horn wound his way back through the confusion. Soon they had plowed through town and parked the wagon next to a faded, unpainted building that sported a crudely painted sign—Jacob's Goods & Services. While Nathan turned the teams out into a nearby corral that sloped dangerously downhill, Push-Bill Horn supervised the unloading of the wagons. By the time Nathan returned, the freighter had emptied the wagons and stuffed his poke with gold.

"What are you going to do with that?" Nathan asked.

"Ship it off to Galena by Wells-Fargo. I don't carry no more than travelin' and repair money. We'll spend the night down at the Colorado House," he announced. "Got a good friend there who always saves me a clean bed."

From what Nathan could see of the crowd at 10, he doubted that there could be anything clean in the whole town. After a brief stop at the freight office, they arrived in front of the Colorado House just as the sun dropped behind the towering mountain to the west. Nathan pushed through the throng and peeked into the window of the two-story, wood-framed building. The entire downstairs was a huge, bolted dining room with long rows of rough-cut tables set with tin plates, forks, and knives. Benches lined each side.

While Nathan was still staring at the place, Push-Bill fought his way back through the crowd on the raised wooden sidewalk and handed him something that looked like a poker chip.

"What's this?" Nathan shouted above the roar.

"It's your supper token," Push-Bill explained. "When you hear the bell ring, shove your way through this mob, hand that to the big man with the gray beard, and then dive for a spot at one of them tables. You start eatin' as fast as you can, and when you hear the bell ring, you got to quit. If you don't stop, you'll get throw'd out on your ear and never be allowed back inside."

"You're joking," Nathan gasped.

"Are you hungry?"

"Yeah!"

"I'm not stretchin' ya, son. So don't come crying to me if you go hungry."

He had barely finished speaking when Nathan heard a faint bell ring and a roar from the crowd of men. It reminded him of his father's descriptions of charging into battle during the war. Now, armed with ravenous appetites, they stormed the tables of the Colorado House.

Nathan didn't bother keeping track of Push-Bill. He tossed his token to a huge, gray-bearded man and dashed to a table. He squeezed in front of an empty tin plate between two very large, dark-skinned men. They looked to Nathan like veterans of many supper battles as they shouted above the roar of the diners, "Waiter, over here. Pork and beans! Coffee! Hot coffee! We got to have bread! Beefsteak! Eggs! More eggs! Potatoes! Where's the potatoes? Gravy!"

Nathan found himself shoving down food as fast as he could scrape it into his mouth. As the two big men kept the food rolling to their table, Nathan crammed down a plateful of cobbler, but in the mass confusion he couldn't tell if it was peach or apple.

As he furiously scraped the fork across his plate, he heard the bell again. Immediately the diners started to exit. Nathan had never viewed such a scene of destruction. Piles of empty dishes, upturned coffeepots, mounds of silverware, bread, meat, and bone fragments littered the tables.

The rough wood floor looked like a city garbage dump as smelly men picked their teeth and belched their way out the door. Though it was now dark and the streets more crowded than ever, Nathan was relieved that supper was over.

Push-Bill Horn grabbed Nathan by the shoulders and dragged him to the edge of the crowd.

"Is it always this way at the Colorado House?"

"Nah," Push-Bill laughed. "It's usually swarmed on a Saturday night. I guess business is trailing off."

"Trailing off?"

"Yep...I remember one run up here, I had to wait out in the street until midnight before I could get to the door."

"I don't understand," Nathan pressed. "Why did we have to hurry out?"

"'Cause they got to clean it up for the next shift, of course. They run six breakfasts, ten dinners, and eight suppers. The man with the gray beard—that's Henry McSwain, probably the richest man in 10."

"Where are we going now?" Nathan asked.

"Out to tend the stock—" Push-Bill stopped to point to the darkening mountain. "Did you see that?"

"What?"

"That lightning. It'll be here in no time."

"Rain in the middle of summer?"

"I mean a gully-washin', snake-drownin', cave-in-producin' downpour like these mountains are famous for."

Nathan studied the murky clouds. "When do you think it will hit?" The air felt heavy to him.

"In about an hour I suppose. Anyway, we'll be holed up in a nice room at the Colorado House by then. I told you McSwain was a friend of mine. We bushwhacked together from St. Louis to Denver. He took his funds and a one-third bonus for not returnin' and disappeared up in the San Juans. Next thing I knew he was a shopkeeper, then a hotel man."

After they cared for the animals, Push-Bill and Nathan tied the tarps down tight on the empty freight wagons. Nathan stored his saddle and personal items in one of the wagons, and Push-Bill tossed his gear in the other. Tona slept under the lead wagon and refused to venture any closer to town.

As they threaded their way back through the crowd, Nathan heard thunder rolls. A few faint drops sprinkled his face. He remembered his own grimy neck and wondered what his mother would think. Or Leah!

One of McSwain's exhausted workers led Push-Bill and Nathan up the outside stairway to the hotel above the restaurant. It opened to the street level above them. Nathan was shocked to step into

44

one gigantic single room. Two hundred fifty wooden boards—two-by-six-foot, propped up like cots and laid out in rows—filled the entire room.

No sheets.

No mattress.

No pillow.

No privacy.

In fact, they couldn't find one empty place.

"We can't sleep here," Nathan groaned. "There's no room."

The worker shrugged. "Just wait a little while. Some of these men have slept all afternoon. As soon as they get up, you can have their beds."

"The lad's right," Push-Bill roared. "I'm a good friend of McSwain's, and he promised me a decent room."

"Oh...well, why didn't you tell me that in the first place? You must be referring to the layout room."

"The what?" Nathan asked.

The worker led them back down the stairs and out to a small rectangular building next to the Colorado House. Two identical front doors framed a twelve-by-twenty-four-foot building which looked to Nathan like two separate hotel rooms.

The man pushed the door open, glanced into the shadows, and pulled it back closed. "That one's full." Then he walked over to the other door and looked inside.

"You're in luck, boys. There's plenty of room here. And only two dollars a night."

In the flickering light of a kerosene lantern that hung near the door Nathan saw a stark, bare, windowless room with absolutely no furnishings.

45

Four men sprawled on bedrolls along the far wall. "Where's the beds?" Nathan asked.

"It's a layout room, I said. You just take your own bedroll and lay it out on the floor anywhere you would like."

"What happened to the beds they used to have in these rooms?" Push-Bill bellowed.

"They got all busted up, so we pulled them out. You going to take it or not?"

"How many men do you cram into this?" Nathan questioned. "Not more than twenty-five. No, sir, McSwain is real particular about that."

"Twenty-five?" Nathan gasped.

Push-Bill glanced at Nathan. "Well, let's you and me sleep in the wagons tonight."

Nathan felt like a man sentenced to hang who had just received a pardon. They raced back to the wagons. A driving rain blasted their faces, and mud clung to their boots. Nathan hunkered into his bedroll, listening to the downpour pound the taut canvas top. This time Tona climbed up into the wagon with him.

Nathan had pulled off his boots, but left the rest of his clothes on. His saddle made a stiff, cold pillow. Tona crawled onto the bedroll at his feet. Nathan was soon asleep.

◆ ◆ ◆ ◆ ◆

It was a crazy dream—like the ones you have right before you wake up in the morning. Nothing made any sense. At first Nathan was riding Onepenny and chasing a bobcat about the size of a steer. When he lassoed the bobcat and pulled the rope to dally it on the saddle horn, the massive

46

animal jumped right up at him knocking him off the saddle. He hit his head on something hard.

In the dream when he came to, he was in a small crowded cabin that belonged to the Rialto sisters. Each wore the same kind of blue calico dress, and each looked quite a bit like Leah.

He entered a small kitchen. There on a very large table were piles and piles of meat, potatoes, carrots, and bread with so much gravy poured over the top of them that it ran off the side of the table and dripped onto the floor.

Suddenly, the Rialto sisters disappeared. Only Leah remained in the room. "Nathan T. Riggins," she commanded. "I want you to eat every bite."

Nathan groaned as he lifted his fork, but was pleasantly surprised to wake up in the wagon, daylight breaking across the top of the canvas.

The storm had ended.

It looked like a clear summer day.

Tona was out exploring.

Nathan's stomach ached from last evening's meal.

His neck felt stiff and smarted.

He yanked on his boots and peered around at the almost- deserted street on the backside of 10. As he climbed down off the wagon, he noticed that the mules and horses anxiously milled around the corral. They all moved toward him, as if expecting to be fed.

I didn't think I'd get up earlier than Push-Bill. Maybe he went down to the Colorado House for breakfast. Not me. I'd rather wait 'til dinner. I'll just eat some jerky...no, I traded that to Washoe Willy.

Nathan looked for tracks in the mud around Push-Bill's wagon to see what direction he had traveled. Finding none at all, he climbed up on the wagon and pulled back the canvas.

"Push-Bill," he cried out. The freighter was tied with ropes and a bandanna gagged his mouth. Nathan pulled down the bandanna and began tugging at the knots in the ropes.

"It's about time you stirred around," Push-Bill shouted. "I was beginning to think you'd leave me in here 'til noon. They's as good as dead...I hope they've said good-bye to their Marys because they are absolutely, thoroughly, completely, without hesitation, unequivocally, exceedingly, comprehensively dead."

"Who?" Nathan implored.

"Those three blackguards who stole my poke, that's who. And I know who they are. Anyway I know one of 'em." Push-Bill Horn dug through his supplies and grabbed a handful of shotgun shells. Pulling his short-barreled scattergun out from a box in the wagon, he turned to Nathan.

"Get that Winchester of yours, boy. It's time to do a man's work."

CHAPTER 4

"**I**'ll kill 'em...I'll kill all three of 'em," Push-Bill raged.

Nathan scurried through the thin crowd of early morning stragglers, chasing after the freighter. His boots felt stiff, and he stepped carefully, trying to avoid the larger mud puddles. He carried his Winchester in one hand and with the other caught hold of Push- Bill's sleeve.

"Push-Bill, wait. Wait up! Couldn't we just tell the town marshal?"

"I don't need no lawman to settle my beefs. Besides, there ain't no lawmen up here."

"None at all?"

"Nope."

"But how do you know who took your money?"

"'Cause he came askin' for a loan, but when I refused, he and those two others got the jump on me."

"Who did it?"

"Quickly."

"Quickly what?"

"The polecat's name is Quickly. But his name is going to be dead—real soon now."

"Is Quickly his first name or last?"

"He only has one name, and it's definitely going to be the last. We was partners up on the Boise."

"And now you're going to kill him?"

"No man steals from Push-Bill Horn...ever!"

"'Vengeance is mine, saith the Lord,'" Nathan quoted. "I read that in the Bible yesterday."

"Well, I figure sometimes the Lord is sort of busy over in other parts of the world and needs us to help level things out," Push-Bill tried to explain. "Anyway, don't you go quoting out of the Good Book at me. I didn't hire no preacher to ride the wagon."

"I'm not going to shoot anyone," Nathan protested.

"You won't need to. Just keep an eye on my back side and don't let anyone sneak up on me. I'll do all the rest."

"Where are we goin'?" Nathan asked.

"To the Bucket of Blood."

"The what?"

"The saloon. It's where Quickly always gambles. Right now he's undoubtedly losing my money. He's a lousy gambler."

"How can you kill a friend?"

"He ain't a friend no more. Besides, it's a matter of principle. If you let one man rob you blind, every fool in the district will try the same. In this country you can't let that happen."

Push-Bill shoved his way into the Bucket of Blood Saloon & Gambling Establishment. Nathan slipped inside the doorway and stood in the shadows against the wall. This Sunday morning the building was almost vacant. Chairs were stacked on the tables, the long wooden bar was empty, and

50

the only light came from outside, beaming through the windows and doors. Dust hung in the air along with the smell of alcohol and stale smoke.

At the back of the room, five men sat around a card table. From their looks, Nathan guessed they'd been playing all night.

Lord, I don't know what I'm doing here. Don't let Push-Bill shoot anyone...and don't let him get hurt...don't let anyone get hurt. That money isn't worth anyone's life.

Push-Bill, holding his shotgun straight in front of him, approached the table. One of the men spotted him. They all stood up, wide-eyed and reaching for their guns.

"Don't try it, boys. This scattergun will hit you all. I want to know where Quickly is, and I want to know right now," Push-Bill shouted.

"Now, Push-Bill, don't get all riled. Quickly's gone south."

"Gone south? What about those two with him?"

"One tall and the other kind of dark?" the man asked.

"Them's the ones," Push-Bill growled.

"They're a hard pair. Quickly paid 'em off, and they claimed they was driftin' up toward Montana."

Push-Bill eased off the scattergun. The men around the table began to relax.

"What do you mean, paid them off?" the freighter asked.

"Old Quickly got slicked out of $300 in a card game. They set him up, but we could never see how they done it. Anyway, they was a threatenin' to shoot him if he didn't raise the money. I guess he lifted yours."

"I'll kill him," Push-Bill insisted.

"Yeah...he kind of figured that. That's why he lit shuck," one of the men at the table added.

Just then a man dressed in a black vest and narrow black tie came in from a back room.

"Push-Bill," he called.

The freighter whirled around, threw the scattergun to his shoulder, and pointed it at the man.

"Whoa...not so fast," the man cautioned. "I've got something for you. Quickly asked me to give this to ya." The man handed him a large certificate.

Push-Bill hesitated and then slowly lowered the gun. He cautiously reached for the large, stiff piece of paper.

"He said it was to pay you back for the loan," the man added.

"Loan? He lifted my poke!" Push-Bill looked the paper over. "One hundred feet in the All-Is-Lost," he roared. "He lifted my poke, and he wants to give me this worthless mining stock? What did he do, find this in the trash?"

"Now...Push-Bill," one of the men soothed him. "That's a mighty rich prospect. Some boys think that'll be the biggest mine in the region if they can get it developed."

"I'll kill him," Push-Bill snarled. "You tell him if he sticks his skinny head into the state of Nevada again, I'll ring his neck like a chicken's and stew him in boiling oil."

"I'll tell him." The man in the vest nodded.

Push-Bill wadded up the mining claim and threw it across the room. As soon as he banged out of the door, Nathan ran to retrieve the claim. He tried to smooth it out and stuffed it into his pocket as he ran after the freighter.

"That's the last night we're sleepin' in 10," Push-Bill announced. "The town's so noisy you can't hear a bushwhacker sneak up on ya. No, sir, I ain't goin' through that again."

"What do we do now?" Nathan asked.

"We hitch up the wagons and hightail it back to Galena for another load."

"What about your money? How much did you lose?"

"$300. But I ain't lost it yet. I told ya, I'll kill Quickly next time I see him. Now let's get some breakfast at the Colorado House. I've still got a couple tokens."

"Is there anyplace else to eat?" Nathan squirmed.

"None that you wouldn't be embarrassed to meet your mama in."

◆ ◆ ◆ ◆ ◆

After a battle for breakfast, Nathan and Push-Bill scooted toward the corrals. Nathan noticed a well-dressed woman holding up her ankle-length skirt to cross the muddy street. He stared a moment. In this town of males, she looked as out of place as a sheepherder at a cowboy convention.

She looks like she's going to ...

"Sunday! This is Sunday, Push-Bill. I promised my mama I'd go to church if we were in town on a Sunday."

53

"Well, there ain't no church in 10."

"Where's that lady going?"

"Oh, them Methodists meet out at a brush arbor for singin' and shoutin'."

"Can I go?" Nathan asked.

"Well, if you trade your rifle for a Bible, they might let you attend. I'll go get some supplies for the return trip."

"You're out of money," Nathan reminded him.

"But I ain't out of credit." Push-Bill stormed down the street.

◆ ◆ ◆ ◆ ◆

At just past 1:00 P.M. Push-Bill and Nathan finally left 10. With the mules rested, the wagons empty, and the trail stretching downhill before them, they moved along at a steady clip. At the first stop Nathan swung down from Onepenny and began to grease the axles. Push-Bill ambled over to him.

"How did you get along with them Methodists?"

Nathan glanced up. "Nice people. One man said we could stay in his cabin if we ever needed a place to sleep. They all said I should come back and bring you with me."

"Me?" Push-Bill bellowed. "I don't fit in with no singin' Methodists."

"Yeah, that's what I told them," Nathan teased.

"You did? Now why'd ya tell them that?"

"Because," Nathan laughed, "I've heard you sing."

54

◆ ◆ ◆ ◆ ◆

The trip back to Galena was routine. No Indians.

No bushwhackers.

No trouble with the mules.

No vagrants selling mining claims.

It was so boring that Nathan shouted with joy at the top of his voice when he caught the first glimpse of the town. After greasing the wheels one last time, he mounted Onepenny and raced to town with Tona leading the way.

His first thought was to race all the way home. However, as he approached town, he decided to take a tour first. Tona cut through an alley and headed to the Riggins house, but Nathan and Onepenny trotted down Main Street.

As he passed by the bank, the front door banged open. A shout blasted out into the street.

"Nathan, when did you get back? Man, you're dirty. Didn't you ever wash? What was 10 like? Did you see any gold? My father says there's lots of gold in that place. What are you doing, Riggins? Are you lost?"

"Colin!" Nathan waved. He rode Onepenny to the rail by the bank and slid to the ground. "I just had to look around at Galena. It's kind of peaceful—did you know that?"

"Peaceful?"

"Compared to 10."

"What's 10 like?"

"It's like payday at the mines, the fourth of July, a riot, a circus, and the confusion we had when Thunder fought the bull—all rolled into one day, and then it repeats itself over and over."

"Did you find any gold?" Colin asked. "Was it lying in the streets and stuff?"

"If they had any streets." Nathan laughed. "The only thing lying in them are drunks and garbage." Nathan looked up and down the sidewalk as he talked.

"I say, Riggins, are you looking for someone?"

"Colin...have you seen Leah?"

"She's probably with good ol' Kylie."

"What? Kylie Collins is here? Actually in Galena?"

Colin threw his arm around Nathan's neck and tugged him toward an alley speaking in a low, hushed voice.

"As a matter of fact, he's been in Galena for a week. The two of them are always together. In the Mercantile, at the livery, in church, over at the bakery...say, did you know the Deluxe has a new baker from San Francisco? You should try the pineapple pastry."

Nathan heard very little of the rest of what Colin said. It was as if someone had slammed a fist into his midsection.

He ached all over.

His stomach cramped.

He felt a little dizzy.

Remounting Onepenny, Nathan left Colin still rambling on about the new cook. He purposely didn't ride past Walker's Barbershop, but took the alley between Slausen's Dry Goods and the faded red siding of the Oriental Cafe. His mother ran out to meet him as he tied Onepenny off in front of the house.

"Nathan, where were you?" She threw her arms around him. "Tona made it home several minutes ago."

"Eh...mother...I'm kind of dirty. You might not want to—"

"Well, I certainly think your mama deserves a hug."

"Yes, ma'am...but couldn't we do that inside?"

"Oh, yes...you wouldn't want anyone to see ..."

"Mother...it's not that," he began. Then his face lapsed into a smile. "Well, actually, it is that, isn't it?"

"Of course it is." She laughed. "Your father is at the office. Did you stop and see him?"

"Not yet."

"Did you eat well on the trip? Was there any trouble? Is it hard work? Or perhaps a little boring? Father said freighting is so slow it would bore him to tears. I hope you kept up your reading. Did you read, Nathan? I hear 10 is awfully wild. A man came through town just the other day with such horrid reports. But I suppose you didn't stay in town long enough to have trouble—just unload and leave. Anyway, you wash up, then come in and tell me everything that happened."

He did.

◆ ◆ ◆ ◆ ◆

Within two hours, Nathan boiled water, took a hot bath, put Onepenny up at the livery, brought wood for the stove, and told his father about the trip.

"Well, I ran across Push-Bill down at the freight office," Marshal Riggins told him. "He said you were the best worker he's had on the trail in five years. I'm proud of you, son. Maybe this summer job will work out real nice."

"Did he mention the problem with Quickly?" Nathan asked. "Yep. Push-Bill's a prideful man...figures it's up to him to settle the score."

Nathan crawled up on the top rail of the corral fence and looked his dad in the eyes. "What will happen next?"

"In time Push-Bill will cool off, but for now don't you go backing his play. Just tell him you got no stake in it and stick to your job. He'll understand. Push-Bill has a lot of sand, but he's not the type to go around shootin' people."

Nathan pushed back his hat. "Unless he gets desperate enough...like Mr. Wobley."

"Pride and desperation can be a tricky combination to handle," the marshal agreed. "Now," he asked grinning, "where are you headed all decked out like a cowboy on a Saturday night?"

"Oh...you mean, the shirt?" Nathan blushed.

His father poked him in the ribs. "I mean, the new green shirt, clean fingernails, hair slicked back."

Nathan jumped down off the rail and scratched the toe of his boot in the dirt. "Well, Leah made this shirt for my birthday, remember? And I was...you know...awful dirty. So I thought I'd just clean up and scout around town."

"Well, if I were you, I'd scout down near the stage office," the marshal suggested.

"Why?" Nathan asked.

"Because that's where I last saw Leah."

"Was she alone?" Nathan pressed.

"Nope."

Nathan wanted to ask more—Was she with Kylie? What does he look like? How was she acting? *And did she ask about me?*

But he said nothing.

Leaving his father, Nathan walked back up to Main Street and turned east. He could see the afternoon stage pulling away in the direction of Battle Mountain Station. He thought he saw a green dress in the crowd.

As he got closer, he spied Leah, still a few blocks away, strolling his direction with her head down. Nathan ducked into the two-foot-wide alley between Cormack's Clock Repair Shoppe and the Eat Here and Die Saloon. After Leah walked by, Nathan crept up behind her.

"Excuse me for being so forward, miss, but that's a beautiful dress."

Breaking out of deep thought, she spun around and stared wide-eyed.

"Nathan, you're home."

"For three days." He smiled. "Where's Kylie?"

"He's gone. You just missed him. He was on the Battle Mountain stage."

"Sorry about that. I heard you two had a real good time."

"Where'd you hear that?" Leah demanded.

"Eh...you know...from Colin."

"Colin don't know nothin' about nothin'."

Nathan tried to study Leah's eyes, but she kept glancing down. "You mean, you and Kylie didn't have a good time?"

"I didn't say that neither," she huffed.

"B-but I thought—Nathan stammered.

59

"Nathan T. Riggins, how come you was gone when you should have been here, and you're here when you should be gone?"

"What?"

"You heard me," she fumed.

"You want me to go?" he asked.

When Leah looked up, tears streamed down her cheeks. "I want you to make up your mind."

"Make up my mind? Make up my mind about what?" Nathan repeated. "Are you crying?"

By now the tears dripped from her cheeks and stained her new green dress.

"No, I ain't crying. And don't you ever go around sayin' I was."

Leah hiked up her long skirt and ran down the sidewalk toward her father's barbershop. For several moments Nathan stood staring blankly down the wooden sidewalk filled with all sorts of people, but not Leah Walker.

◆ ◆ ◆ ◆ ◆

Nathan saw her only once more in the next three days. She seemed to be avoiding him.

Lord, I don't understand. Nowadays every time I talk to her, she runs away crying. We didn't used to have to have a reason to see each other. We just sort of talked and played and ran and laughed. But now it's different. It's like every conversation has to be important. I want to grow up, but I don't want to give up having fun.

"Let's roll 'em out," Push-Bill shouted at 6:00 a.m.

Dust hung heavy in the air. Nathan couldn't see a cloud in the sky. The slight breeze felt warm.

60

As they wound their way past the last few buildings of the city, he smelled bacon blended with the aroma of the sagebrush. Tona trotted beside Onepenny. Both appeared happy to be once more making tracks.

On the first trip out it had all seemed like a great adventure.

Now it just felt like work.

And this time Nathan didn't look back as they left Galena behind.

CHAPTER 5

Nathan spent the first day out thinking mostly of Leah—about how they always argued and how he missed her in spite of it. He thought about how pretty her hair looked all summer. And how warm her hand felt when he held it.

He spent the second day thinking about dust and heat, thirst and bushwhackers, vengeance and justice. And gold.

They pulled into Bobcat Springs in the late afternoon and soon had the animals tended and camp organized. Right after licking up the remnants of Nathan's second plate of beans, Tona disappeared into the rocks west of the springs.

Push-Bill Horn sat back from the small fire and loaded his pipe. "Did I ever tell you about the time me and Jim Bridger went elk huntin' up on the Yellowstone?" he quizzed.

"I reckon you didn't," Nathan said with a wide grin.

"Well, son...it was in late October of the year, and we was looking forward to hanging some elk for the winter. So ol' Gabe and me followed sign up over a steep ridge that neither of us had ever crossed. Now we had just hiked out of the trees into a clearin' when we spotted him. Standing not more than a hundred feet away was the biggest bull elk I'd ever seen. I was already frettin' on how we would ever carry it back to camp.

"Well, ol' Jim, he wants to take it, so he throws his rifle to his shoulder and fires a round. Now Jim Bridger was a mighty fine shot, and I was shocked to see that he had completely missed the elk. Jim was furious, but startled, because that elk didn't even flinch. It didn't bolt, jump, or even look our way. About now I'm figurin' we ran across a deaf elk.

"So Jim, he loads her up and takes aim for another go. I watch in disbelief as he misses that elk again. I start to shoot the thing myself, but ol' Jim is so sure enough furious that he charges right at the elk, plannin' on hitting it over the head with the barrel of his rifle.

"Well, son...Jim hadn't run twenty feet until he runs face first into a solid glass mountain. It was just like that black obsidian, but this here was a rare, clear obsidian. No wonder he couldn't hit the thing. But not only that, the glass mountain acted as a magnifier. And instead of that elk bein' a hundred feet, we figure it was more like twenty miles away.

"If you ever get up into the Yellowstone, make sure you look up that glass mountain 'Course you can't see it, but you can run into it, that's certain sure."

By the time Push-Bill finished his story, Nathan was doubling over with laughter. He was trying to grab enough air to talk when Tona's piercing cry sent shivers down his back.

"Tona's hurt," Nathan yelled. He grabbed his carbine out of the scabbard and raced around the springs.

Not a snake bite again! Please, Lord, don't let him get bitten by a snake.

Nathan leaped over some boulders, his left foot coming down on loose gravel, and he tumbled into the rocks. The Winchester crashed into the granite, and he reached out to break the fall with his right hand.

Slamming into the rocks, he felt the skin rip away on the palm of his hand. He staggered to his feet and clutched his wound. It felt as if he had dragged it through a cactus patch. Brushing back tears and smearing blood on his face, he searched for his carbine and then raced toward the Tona's shrieks.

Stumbling over the crest of the rocks, Nathan spotted Tona flung on his back down among the boulders. Standing over him was a bobcat. The animal had ripped Tona's thigh, a jagged ugly wound, and would have torn off the leg completely had it not been for Nathan's approach.

The animal's eyes blazed at Nathan. He slammed the carbine to his shoulder and grabbed the trigger guard lever to cock the gun. The fierce pain in his hand prevented him from setting the jammed lever.

It's stuck. It got jammed in the fall.

He charged the bobcat, hoping to clobber it with his carbine barrel, but the animal darted out of sight, leaving the wounded Tona behind.

"Tona," Nathan sobbed. "Tona!" He bent down low to lift the animal out of the rocks, and the gray and white dog viciously snapped at him.

"Tona, it's me, Nathan. I'll help you, boy."

Laboring for breath, Tona growled at Nathan.

"It's all over for him. Let me put him down, son."

Push-Bill towered on the crest of the rocks, revolver in hand.

"No," Nathan pleaded. "No! He'll pull through. I know he will." The tears flowed so heavy now he couldn't see clearly.

"Son...you got to put him out of his pain...it ain't fair. You go on back and I'll..."

"No! You're not killing my dog," Nathan shouted. "Come help me. We've got to get him back to camp. Help me, Push-Bill...please!"

Push-Bill Horn holstered his gun and, with a speed that amazed Nathan, grabbed Tona's nose and clamped the dog's jaws shut. Then with a gentleness that didn't seem to fit his big, calloused hands, he picked the bleeding dog up and began to carry him back to camp.

Scrambling to keep up, Nathan wrapped his bandanna around his own bleeding hand. Push-Bill laid the dog by the fire and gently folded the ripped hindquarters back to its original position.

"It's tom to the bone, son...I'm mighty sorry, but you've got to help him out. He's been too good a dog to let him go on and suffer."

Tona was silent, struggling for every short breath.

"No, I can't, Push-Bill, don't ya see? I just can't. Isn't there anything we could do?" Nathan pleaded.

"Well...a man could always pour whiskey in the wound and sew it up...but I ain't got a drink, and I don't have no needle and thread."

Nathan searched around wildly with his eyes. "How about in the wagon?"

65

"Son, them goods is buttoned down tight. I can't go spreading them across the desert lookin' for somethin' that might not even be there."

"We have to do something." Nathan's hands and arms began to shake, and he couldn't make them stop. He felt like a person who was being held under water against his will.

Push-Bill grabbed him by the shoulders and shook him hard.

"Nate, you listen to me. Get hold of yourself. You got to let go. The good Lord don't let us keep them animals forever. It was bound to happen sometime. Let him go, son...let him go!"

"No," Nathan sobbed. "I can't. I just...won't!"

Push-Bill threw his big arm around Nathan's shoulder and let out a deep sigh. "Son, we'll wrap them wounds up tight with some rags. Then you pour some water into his mouth every half-hour or so...if he's alive in the morning, we'll put him under the belly of that wagon with the firewood and take him with us."

By dark Tona was wrapped in a sack that read "Quaker Mills, Akron, Ohio." Nathan's hand displayed a clean bandanna, and Push-Bill had straightened the hammer on his Winchester carbine.

Nathan had a little cup of water by the sleeping dog, and every half-hour he forced Tona's mouth open and poured in a teaspoon or so.

Push-Bill broke a long silence.

"Son...you got to remember that Tona's just a dog. He got hurt doin' exactly what dogs are born to do—chasin' a cat."

"It isn't fair. I should have kept him at home."

"In a pen? Now that wouldn't have been fair. Dogs is meant to roam and explore and get themselves into mischief."

"If I had it to do all over again, I'd still leave him at home."

"And if that dog had it to do all over again, he'd go right back after that bobcat. But life don't back up. It just rolls on."

Nathan tried to stay awake to keep Tona from dehydrating, but around midnight he slipped off to sleep. A couple of times during the night, he heard a noise and woke up enough to see Push-Bill giving Tona a drink.

Right before sunup, Nathan stole out of his bedroll, pulled on his boots, checked on Tona, grabbed his carbine, and slipped out into the rocks next to the springs.

Ninety minutes and two shots later, he shuffled back into camp. The sun blazed over the eastern mountains, and Push-Bill was beginning to hitch the team.

"Where's Tona?" Nathan shouted. "He didn't...You didn't..."

"He's barely alive, so I tucked him on top of the firewood."

"Will he make it to 10?"

"Only the Lord can give you that answer," Push-Bill declared. "I suppose you were bobcat huntin'?"

"Yep. I'm going to kill him."

"You mean, you didn't have any luck jist now?"

"Nope. I never even saw him."

"Then why are you so dead set at killin' him?"

"It's a matter of principle. It's a matter of justice. An eye for an eye...and all that."

"Well, now...I believe the Good Book was written for people—not critters. Besides, that dog ain't dead yet."

"It doesn't matter," Nathan insisted. "I'm going to kill that bobcat anyway."

"'Vengeance is mine, saith the Lord.' Seems like a lad told me that recently," Push-Bill reminded him.

Lord, just let me have one clean shot at that cat.

"This is different," Nathan insisted.

A few miles out of Bobcat Springs, Nathan spotted trees against the base of the distant mountains.

"Is that the Rialto ranch?" he asked.

"Yep."

"I'll bet they have needle and thread—maybe even some alcohol for the wound."

"I reckon they do, but we cain't pull over there now. I've got to keep these wagons rollin' to 10."

"Let me carry Tona over there on Onepenny."

"We got to move on up the trail."

"I'll catch up. You just keep them rolling. Please."

"I don't know if I should turn you loose with that band of girls."

"I won't pester them, honest," Nathan pleaded.

"It weren't them that I was worried about," Push-Bill explained. "But if the wounds don't kill the mutt, the dust under that wagon will. I'll let you go,

but you got to catch up by midafternoon...ya
hear?"

"Yes, sir," Nathan shouted, jumping off
Onepenny to gently retrieve his dog.

Tona didn't protest. He didn't open his eyes.
His tongue and his nose were both dry and caked
with dust. Nathan poured a little water into the
dog's mouth, and Tona tried to swallow, then gave
up, coughed, and drooled most of the water out
the side of his mouth.

The dog cradled in his lap, Nathan pulled off
the trail and rode toward the distant trees. His
mind drifted back to when Tona first followed him
into Willow Creek. For a while he relived all the
events of the preceding year. Abruptly, he came
back to the present.

What had looked like a flat valley all the way
to the ranch now dropped down into a ravine.

*Lord, you've just got to help Tona. I need
him. Sometimes it seems like he's my best friend.
We've been through everything together. Bears
and snakes, outlaws and coyotes, bulls and
blizzards. Not to mention buffaloes. Please, Lord!*

Climbing out of the dry, ancient riverbed,
Nathan studied the trees. They seemed even
further away now than when he had begun.

*One other thing, Lord. Help me kill that
bobcat. I want justice. Just give me a chance to
even the score.*

Nathan calculated it took over an hour more
to come close enough to see any buildings near the
Rialto ranch. He was surprised to discover that the
trees were not cottonwoods scattered along a
creek or spring, but rather a row of scrub cedars.
They'd been carefully planted beside a mile-long

drive that led to a neatly maintained two-story house.

Tona hadn't opened his eyes for several miles. Nathan constantly searched the dog's neck for a heartbeat.

"Hang on, boy...you've got to hang on!"

He had ridden about halfway up the drive when a girl's voice from behind caused him to jump.

"What you want, boy?"

He spun around and glanced down the barrel of a shotgun perched on the shoulder of a brown-haired girl who looked about his age.

"Eh...is this...is this the Rialto ranch?"

"Maybe it is and maybe it isn't. What do you want?"

"Look, my dog got ripped up by a bobcat back at the springs. I need to get him fixed up and thought maybe you could help."

The girl, clothed in a faded dress with the sleeves pushed up to the elbows, stepped up to Nathan but didn't lower her gun. "What's that dog's name?"

"Tona."

"Tona? That's a dumb name," she announced. Then she lowered the gun a little and stepped up to look. "He's hurt bad, isn't he?"

"Yeah. Can I get some help?"

"Maybe...it's up to Sal. You walk that horse to the house and keep those hands in front of you. You try to pull a gun, and I'll blow you out of that saddle quicker than you can blink." Then she turned to the cedars and hollered, "Come on, girls, let's take him home."

Three younger girls stepped out of the trees. The two oldest looking ones also carried guns. All three wore long, yellow calico dresses.

"What's his name, Nan?" the tallest of the three, with ink- black air, asked.

"Boy, what's your name?" the leader quizzed.

"Nathan. Nathan T. Riggins from Galena. Eh, what's your name?"

"We're Rialtos," she informed him.

"I'm Jerri," the black-haired one offered.

"And I'm Nina," the little blonde girl added.

The smallest took off running toward the house and shouted back, "I'm Babylon, but everyone calls me Babe."

"Babylon?" Nathan mumbled.

"What of it?" Nan growled.

They traveled several more minutes without speaking. Nathan glanced occasionally at the girls who whispered and giggled as they skipped along beside him. Finally, black-haired Jerri tugged at his pant leg.

"Hey, boy...how old are you?"

"Thirteen."

"When's your birthday?"

"A couple weeks ago. Why?"

"He belongs to Cape." Nina giggled.

"Cape?"

"She's our sister," Nina answered. "I told you he was too old for you, Jerri."

"Well," Jerri huffed, "he's too young for Nan."

"And he's too skinny," Nan added, never lowering her shotgun. Nathan arrived in the well-kept yard of the Rialto ranch with Tona still in his lap. To the side were two large barns, corrals with several animals, a chicken coop, and a

71

smokehouse. Out back he thought he saw a large garden and some fruit trees. Standing on the front porch was the little brown-haired girl called Babe and two other girls.

Glancing at the oldest of the girls, who looked to Nathan to be about sixteen, he said, "I've got a dog that's ripped up pretty bad, and I was wondering if anyone here could help get him stitched up?"

"He's yours, Cape," Nina shouted. "He's thirteen, and Jerri's too young."

A blonde-haired girl with blue-green eyes squinted into the morning sun and stared at him. She didn't say anything, but turned to the front door of the house.

"Go get Sal," the oldest called to her. Then she turned to the others. "Nina, you take Babe and fetch some water so this boy can wash up. Looks to me like his hand is bleeding. Jerri, go dig him out something to eat. Nan, you take his horse out to the barn. Boy—"

"My name's Nathan T. Riggins."

She walked over to him. "Boy," she emphasized, "give me that dog." Tenderly carrying Tona, she climbed up on the porch with Nathan following behind. As they reached the top step, the front door swung open, and a young woman who looked a lot like Miss D'Imperio, rushed out carrying several empty flour sacks.

"Here," she commanded. "Lay him here, Beth, go fetch the rubbing alcohol. Cape, bring my sewing kit. Where's Nan?"

"She's putting that spotted horse of his away."

"Well, then...after you fetch the sewing kit, bring a little cup of that soup off the stove for the dog."

"It ain't done yet."

"It isn't done," she corrected. "But this dog won't mind, I assure you."

"A bobcat did this?" she asked as she cleaned out the wound with a clean cloth and alcohol.

"Yes, ma'am."

"Please call me Sal," she requested.

"I'm Nathan."

"I know...the girls told me everything. You might not want to watch this," she suggested.

Nathan, starting to feel sick to his stomach, turned away from watching. "I think you're right."

"Your dog's lost a lot of blood."

"Yeah...I know, Miss...Miss Sal."

"If he has any chance of living, he'll need constant rest. I'm going to sew him up now. I don't suppose you have any preference on what color thread I use. Here's a charcoal gray...this should work."

While he was waiting, the girl named Cape brought him a plate of fried eggs and homemade bread, thick with butter. She handed it to him without speaking and returned to the house.

He went over to the recently filled wash basin on the porch, cleaned his face and hands, and then sat down to eat the meal. About the time he finished, all the girls gathered on the front porch as Sal tied off the last of the stitches. She tried to force some warm stew juice down Tona's throat.

"Do you think he'll pull through?" Nathan asked.

"That depends on how much blood he's lost, whether that wound's clean, how much fight he has left in him, and what the Lord wants to do with him."

Sal stood up, brushed out her apron, and then came over to the steps to sit down next to Nathan.

"Now...," she said with a sigh, "who are you, and what in the world are you doing out here?"

"I'm Nathan T. Riggins. I live in Galena with my parents. My father's the marshal there. I'm working for a freighter this summer, greasing axles and tending his livestock. We're hauling goods up to 10. Did you know about the town of 10?"

"Yes," she said nodding.

"Well, we were back there at Bobcat Springs when my dog, Tona—"

"Is that Shoshone?"

"Yes, ma'am...eh, Miss Sal. Anyway, he got tore up by that cat in a fight, and I was desperate to find some help for him. So I hope I didn't impose too much. Now I'll load him up and be on my way."

"You'll do nothing of the kind," she replied.

"What?"

"You'll have to stay for dinner. To do less would be to insult the Rialto name."

"But you just fed me."

"That was merely a snack."

"I've got to get back to the wagons."

"We'll show you a shortcut to 10."

"You've been there?"

"A couple of times a year. We go up and sell our sewn goods and produce."

74

"You haven't told me your story," Nathan prodded.

"Well," Sal began. "I'll let Beth tell you. I need to cook. Besides, she's our schoolteacher anyway."

The tall, brown-haired Beth stepped out into the yard so she could turn to face Nathan. The five other girls scampered down and sat on the steps next to Nathan. The one called Cape sat closest.

"All of us were born right here in this house. But Mama died when Babe was born. Then three winters back Father got stuck out in a blizzard and froze to death. Well, we talked it over for a long, long time and decided this is right where we wanted to stay. So we just divided up the chores and settled in. We don't get much company, but we don't get bothered either."

"Yeah," Babe reported, "if anyone tries something on us—boom! Nan blasts them."

"I haven't shot anyone yet," Nan protested. "But we sure enough scared a few."

"So," Nathan asked, "who does what chores?"

"Well," Beth reported, "Sal's eighteen, so she's the boss. She does most of the cooking, looks after the house, does the doctoring when we're sick, and makes sure we take baths."

"And she reads the Bible to us and prays," Babe chimed in. "I'm next, at sixteen, and my job is to teach the others. We have school everyday. We can all read, write, and do mathematics."

"Plus Beth is teaching us Latin," Cape reported.

"Latin? Where did you learn that?" he asked Beth.

"From my mother. She went to school in New England. Also, I'm helping them all learn how to sew. Then there's Nan—she's fourteen, and she's in charge of the barnyard animals."

"I help her," Nina blurted out.

"Nan milks the cows, pulls calves, smokes the hams—"

"And I do most of the butchering," Nan boasted.

"Then there's Cape—she's twelve, and she's our cowgirl. We've got twenty-two head of cattle and sixteen sheep. She drives them out to pasture and rounds them up to bring them back at night."

"I help her, too," Nina offered.

"Jerri here is ten, and she's taken over the gardening chores. She had to plant, weed, carry water, and pick the garden."

"I'm next," Nina called out.

"And Nina, the bashful eight-year-old—she's everybody's helper. She likes being outdoors, so she helps most often with the animals."

"Don't forget me," Babe insisted.

"And Babe...well, she's a very mature six. Her job is to gather eggs and bring in firewood for the stove."

"Now you know all about us," Nina added. "But Cape still don't like you."

"Nina," Cape fumed. She stomped to her feet and ran back into the house.

"There's one thing I don't know," Nathan ventured. "How did you get your names? Did I hear Babe say her name was Babylon?"

Beth broke into a wide smile. "Yes...mother and father gave us all Biblical names. Sal is really named Jerusalem. I'm not Beth, but Bethlehem.

Nan is for Nazareth. Cape is for Capernaum, Jerri for Jericho, Nina for Ninevah, and you already know about Babe."

"Yeah," Nina bubbled, "coming here is like visiting the whole Bible."

♦ ♦ ♦ ♦ ♦

The immense dining room was spotless, and the linen-covered table piled with food when they all sat down to dinner and waited for Sal to say prayers. Nathan figured the only woman on earth who could cook better than Sal was his mother, and even that was very close.

After dinner and lots of talk and giggles, Nan brought up Onepenny, and Nathan prepared to leave.

"You can't take Tona," Sal reported. "If he has any chance of living, he's got to stay here a while."

"I sure do appreciate it." Nathan tipped his hat after he sat down in the saddle. "I'll check on him next time through."

"We shall look forward to your visit, Nathan T. Riggins," Sal added.

He had turned Onepenny to the east when Nina yelled out, "Nathan, do you have a girlfriend back in town?"

"Eh...sort of...I think," he stammered.

"See, I told you I didn't like him," Cape huffed as she turned her back on him.

The other six Rialto sisters waved until he could no longer see them.

◆ ◆ ◆ ◆ ◆

Nathan knew he was late, but Onepenny was well watered and rested, so he rode hard along the shortcut that Miss Sal had described. Right before sunset he caught sight of the wagons camped in Wild Horse Meadow. Actually he heard gunfire before he spotted the wagons.

Holding his Winchester in his lap, he approached with caution, getting close enough to hear shouting.

"If there was a tree within ten miles, I'd hang you right now." A man was tied spread-eagle to the large rear wheel of one of the freight wagons.

Is this Quickly? Looks like Push-Bill's caught up with him.

CHAPTER 6

"It's about time you showed up, Nate," Push-Bill
hollered. "Hop down and grease them wheels.
Then tend to the mules."

Nathan pointed at the man strapped to the
wheel. "Is that Mr. Quickly?"

Push-Bill nodded. "But that there is not a
mister. That's a dead duck."

"Son," the man shouted at Nathan. "Talk to
Push-Bill, will ya? He seems to be a tad riled."

"Riled, am I? Oh, no. I get riled if a mule
runs off at night. I get riled if an axle breaks. I get
riled if someone tries to make me lower my prices
on the goods...but this! The entire Apache Nation
has never been this mad. You'd be better off being
Custer in the hands of the Sioux. Quickly, you'll
hang on the first tree you see between here and
10."

"Son...talk to him," Quickly pleaded. "I
offered to pay him back the money—and more."

Nathan pulled the saddle off Onepenny and
walked closer to Quickly. "What do you mean you
offered to repay?"

"I came ridin' right up to camp on my own
and offered him $500."

"I thought you only stole $300."

"I think of it as a loan," the man corrected
him. "And Push- Bill is entitled to interest."

"He didn't offer me nothin'," Push-Bill bellowed from near the smoking campfire.

"I offered you $500 and you know it." Quickly howled. Nathan pulled the bandanna off his hand, examined his wound, and then glanced at Push-Bill.

"He rode in here and said he'd pay me $500 for that phony mining stock he gave me. Then when I jumped him and demanded my money, he said he wanted to buy back the stock on credit."

"What?" Nathan exclaimed.

"He don't have a penny to his name," Push-Bill insisted. "I done searched him."

"Look, I had a man offer me $500 for my stock. So I hurried down to find Push-Bill. I'll take the stock and ride back to 10. Then I can cash it in and have the money waiting when you two roll into town."

"You mean there's some value in that stock?" Nathan asked. "At least this old boy thinks so," Quickly called out.

"Well...it don't matter, because I don't have the certificate. I chucked it on the floor of the Bucket of Blood...and besides you ain't never goin' to live to see 10 again."

"Wait a minute," Nathan cried. "You came riding into the camp of a man you bushwhacked and wanted to buy back gold stock on credit? You've got to be the craziest man I ever met."

"I didn't want to bushwhack him. It was those two that cheated me. They was goin' to kill me...and Push-Bill too."

Push-Bill pulled out his revolver and waved it under the bound man's nose. "You should have let 'em kill ya. It would be a might more pleasant than what I aim fer ya."

"Wait," Nathan called. "I've got the stock certificate. It's in my saddlebag. I just remembered. I snatched it up when Push-Bill throw'd it down."

Push-Bill spun back toward Nathan. "You did?"

"Go and see, boy. It's powerful important," Quickly pressured.

Nathan dug through the papers which included the scraps of mining claims he had purchased from the man near Bobcat Springs.

"Here it is. One hundred feet of the All-Is-Lost Mine," Nathan shouted.

"That's it," Quickly yelled. "Now just untie me and let me ride up to 10 and get your money."

"You ain't goin' nowhere," Push-Bill commanded. "You done robbed me once. You ain't goin' to rob me again."

Nathan handed the paper to the freighter. "Maybe we ought to just tow Mr. Quickly along with us. Then you could go with him and get your money when he sells the certificate."

Push-Bill threw a handful of coffee into the pot on the fire and nodded at Nathan. "I was just startin' to think the same thing, son. That way if it's all a big stretcher, I can hang him from the cross beam at the Colorado House."

"No, no! You can't do that," Quickly protested. "If I don't get back there by tomorrow night, I'll lose the sale. We don't have time to wait for these mules. You've got to let me go, Push-Bill. I won't let you down this time."

"You worthless snake-eyed skunk. I'm not untyin' ya until I get my money, or you're hangin' from a tree."

81

"Look, there won't be any money for that certificate if you don't let me go back now. You got my word on it. I swear...I swear...on Kit Carson's grave. I'll do it!"

Push-Bill rubbed his whiskers, stirred the fire, and stared at the flames.

The long silence was broken by Quickly.

"Son...you've got to believe me. If I'm not back, I lose the sale. Talk to him."

"It isn't my hand to play." Nathan shrugged.

Lord...there's got to be a solution that doesn't involve anyone dying. Help Push-Bill deal with his temper.

Nathan tied the horses and mules to the picket line and unloaded the food boxes while Push-Bill continued to gaze at the fire. He couldn't tell if it was the calm before the storm or the calm after it.

It was getting dark when Nathan finally spoke up. "Push-Bill, do you want me to cook some supper?"

"Huh? Oh...no, I'm the cook. I'll do it."

The old freighter pulled out his Green River knife and cut two slabs of salt pork for the frying pan.

"There's three of us, Push-Bill." Nathan nodded at Quickly, still tied to the wagon wheel.

"Oh...yeah." He nodded and cut a third slice without protest.

"You been staring at that fire an awful long time," Nathan prodded.

"Son...did you ever read about Kit?"

"Yes, sir, I did. He got sick and died down in New Mexico after he took that big trip to Washington, didn't he?" Nathan asked.

82

"He died in southern Colorado actually."
Push-Bill nodded. "Well, one time...years ago when
we was young and raw, me, Dirty Ed McGinnis,
Reynolds, and Quickly there...left Ft. Hall to go up
into Blackfeet country and look for gold on a creek
where Quickly claimed he knew an old boy who
picked up nuggets as big as your thumb.

"Anyway...everyone at the fort told us not to
go, that the Blackfeet would murder us the first
night out. Well, we was too mountain-dumb to
know better so we go ridin' off.

"Three days out we come over a draw, and
about fifty Blackfeet meet us lookin' for war. We
made a run for the rocks, but they shot my horse
out from under me. I hollered, but the others was
too far ahead and too scared to hear.

"I started runnin' across the prairie and
wonderin' if I ought to blow my own brains out so I
don't have to face no torture when a rider in
buckskins comes thunderin' down from the bluff.
He fired at the Blackfeet, and they reined up like
they was facing the whole army.

"The man in buckskins reached down and
pulled me up behind him. We cut a nine in our tails
and rode for the rocks with the others. Well, son,
we held out for three days, and then them Indians
just up and disappeared. So we lit shuck for Ft.
Hall."

"Was the man who rescued you Kit Carson?"
Nathan asked.

"Yep. He came into Ft. Hall after we had left
and heard that four crazy greenhorns had rode off
into Blackfeet country, so he headed out to turn us
back. There just weren't many men like ol' Kit, no

sir. So when Quickly there swore on Kit's grave...well, it just caused me to do some thinkin'."

"You think that claim really is good then?" Nathan asked.

"Yep...I reckon it is."

"So are you goin' to let me go on back up to 10 and sell it?" Quickly clamored.

Push-Bill turned to the man tied to the wheel. "No," he shouted.

"But...I thought...," Nathan stammered.

"I'll tell you what I am goin' to do, Nate. I'm goin' to send you and the spotted horse on up to 10 with the certificate. You sell it to the man and then wait at the Colorado House until I get to town."

"You can't do that," Quickly protested. "He don't know who the buyer is."

"Don't matter." Push-Bill insisted. "If one man will pay $500 for it, so will another. He can just peddle it on the street."

"No, you won't get top dollar for it. Don't you see? It ain't general knowledge how rich that strike is. They might not want to buy it at all. I've got to go."

"You ain't goin'," Push-Bill insisted. "So either you tell Nathan where to find your buyer, or he'll sell it on the street."

"You're not serious?" Quickly started to protest, but his voice trailed off. Determination ruled Push-Bill's eyes. "How do you know you can trust the kid? Maybe he'll sell it and then ride on off himself."

Push-Bill's piercing brown eyes blazed into Nathan's. "You goin' to steal my money, Nate?"

"No, sir, I'm not going to steal it."

"There, Quickly. There's still some of us that
is good to our word."

"He'll have to ride all night," Quickly
complained. "He don't know the trail."

"He's got a good horse," Push-Bill responded.

By the time supper was finished, the details
of the plan were settled. Nathan was to ride
straight through to 10, stopping only to rest
Onepenny. Once he got to town he would go to the
Colorado House Cafe and ask for Chance Aragon,
make the sale, hang around town until Onepenny
rested, and then ride back out and meet them on
the trail.

Mounted on Onepenny, Nathan turned back
to Push-Bill.

"You promise you won't kill Mr. Quickly while
I'm gone?" Nathan asked.

"I won't kill him," Push-Bill assured him,
"unless the polecat tries to escape."

"Mr. Quickly, you aren't going to try to
escape, are you?"

"You got my word on it, son," Quickly replied.

"His word ain't worth a wet buffalo chip,"
Push-Bill scoffed.

"Don't take a penny less than $500 for that
claim, keep an eye out for the Shoshone and
Bannocks, and don't take no chances with pilgrims
on the road. If they think you have anything
valuable, they'd just as soon relieve you of it."

"Yes, sir...I can do it," Nathan insisted.

◆ ◆ ◆ ◆ ◆

He hadn't ridden thirty minutes in the dark shadows of early nightfall before he began to question his wisdom.

Lord, I'm...well, I'm not doing this for me. I just want to do what's square for both Push-Bill and Quickly. Nobody ought to lose their life over this...especially me!

Nathan pulled his Winchester out of the scabbard and laid it across his lap as he rode along.

"It could be worse, boy." He leaned over the saddle horn and patted Onepenny's neck. "The moon's almost full...there are no clouds...the breeze is fairly warm so far...I can see the road. There's no dark forest or trees to ride through. We could see someone if they were riding along, couldn't we, boy?"

And they could see us. What if there are Indians? Or outlaws? Or wild animals like...like...no, I guess not.

What about Onepenny tripping and falling? I could get smashed in the rocks. Or I could fall asleep and tumble down a canyon and break my leg. And no one would find me...and I'd be lying there in pain for days, and the ants would crawl all over me and...

A sudden chill shot up Nathan's back.

"Maybe I'll grab my coat when I stop to let you rest," he said to the horse. "What's that up there?" he whispered and pulled up on the reins. Leaning with his face against Onepenny's neck, he studied the dark silhouette on the ridge of mountains to the west.

"It's probably just a boulder or sage or something." He spurred Onepenny, and again they loped down the trail.

86

Nathan rode for what he guessed was about two hours. Then he climbed down, loosened the cinch to allow some air to flow under the saddle, and walked along leading Onepenny by the reins.

He carried the Winchester over his shoulder. Even in the darkness he saw Onepenny's ears suddenly twitch and point forward. He thought he heard hoofbeats in the distance.

"What is it?" he whispered. "Is a horse coming, boy? Come on, let's get off the road."

Nathan led Onepenny off to the side and down into the dark shadows of a ravine where he could still view the road in the moonlight. As he waited, he pulled on his jacket.

Now Nathan heard nothing at all. So he waited a little longer.

And a little longer.

Finally, when Onepenny began to doze off, Nathan jerked the cinch tight and remounted. Back out on the road, he noticed the wind had picked up and now whistled through the barren hills.

It was on this third cycle of walking Onepenny that he spotted movement on the high western slope. It was just a slight motion. Then a soft noise. Then another movement in the shadows.

Lord, I don't know what's up there, but I can't hide this time. There's no cover. Whatever it is must know I'm here. Lord, help me!

Nathan couldn't tell if the object was man or animal, and he couldn't tell if it was getting closer— or staying the same distance. Even though his forehead was cold, sweat rolled down his face. He pulled off his hat and brushed his eyebrows, forehead, and hair on the sleeve of his jacket.

Lord, I've got to do something!

Nathan slowly cocked the lever on his Winchester. Then without much thought and still with his finger on the trigger, he raised the gun high in the air over his head.

If that's a person, at least he ought to know I have a gun and am ready to use it.

On a ridge about 200 feet to the west, the silhouette of a braided rider appeared against the night sky.

Indian!

The rider held a rifle above his head and waved it back and forth. Then he turned and rode over the crest of the mountain away from Nathan.

He's leaving. He had a cocked rifle, too. Maybe he was worried about what I would do. Lord, do Indians ever get scared at night? I sure would like to see some daylight. Do you suppose you could hurry this along?

Nathan figured it was at least another long, numbing hour before the sky turned a lighter shade of dark...then charcoal gray...then a light gray...a pale washed-out blue...and finally the sun rested on the eastern mountains, and the sky turned blue.

Thanks, Lord. I'm glad You don't go to sleep.

◆ ◆ ◆ ◆ ◆

The sun was straight up when Nathan first spotted 10 clinging to the side of White Eagle Mountain.

"That-a-boy. We made good time...look at that."

All morning they'd been passing a string of people and wagons still flooding into the mining town and a trickle of folks leaving it. He nodded, but spoke to no one. He walked Onepenny most of the way up the steep road, but remounted to enter town so that he might look across the crowds of people and find his way to the Colorado House.

"Now how in the world am I going to find someone named Chance Aragon?" he mumbled in the confusion of the crowd that had lined up to attack the midday dinner at the hotel cafe.

Mr. McSwain! I'll go up to McSwain when he comes out to collect dinner tokens, and ask him.

Nathan hung back of the crowd and allowed them to stampede through the doorway as the cafe opened for the next shift. Then, as the hired help tried to cut off the surging throng, Nathan scooted up to the gray-bearded man who was holding a flour sack full of tokens in his hand.

"Mr. McSwain," he shouted, "I work for Push-Bill, and I'm looking for a man named Chance Aragon."

"You ain't goin' to find him here. You got a token?"

"No, I don't want dinner. I want to find Mr. Aragon."

"Check up on the top of City Street. If you don't have a token, you don't eat, son."

By the time he finished the sentence, Nathan was back out in the street and climbing up on Onepenny. "Man, there's no way I'm going to eat there again." He spurred his way through the crowd.

Nathan remembered that the place where they had unloaded the wagons was on City Street, but he couldn't remember what was above the corrals. As he turned up the mountain, the crowd

89

thinned, and he saw several men unloading a freight wagon. One of the men glanced up at Nathan.

"Hey, do you work with Push-Bill?"

"Yeah," Nathan hollered back.

"Did he make it back already?"

Nathan rode closer to the man. "Nope, he sent me ahead. He'll be here tomorrow."

"Well, tell him I'll pay double what I paid last time."

"Double?"

"Yep."

"Why?"

"Prices went up, that's why. They struck pay dirt in one of the mines."

"Which one?" Nathan asked.

"There was an explosion at the Antelope Flats Mine. One man died, but it uncovered a huge vein."

"Antelope Flats? Where's that?"

"Over near the All-Is-Lost."

"Listen, speaking of the All-Is-Lost, I'm looking for Chance Aragon. I heard he was up at the top of City Street."

The man's mouth dropped open. "Eh...yeah, I guess you could say that."

"What's up there anyway?" Nathan quizzed.

"The cemetery." The man shrugged.

"Cemetery? He's dead?"

"Yep. He's the one that got killed in the mine. Some say it wasn't an accident...anyway there's no time to investigate."

"But...I need to see him. I'm supposed to sell him ..."

"Sorry, son, he's dead, but I'll buy all of Push-Bill's goods."

"No, this was, eh...a mining claim."

"Which mine?"

"Eh...the All-Is-Lost."

"That's too bad. Antelope Flats is going for $500 a foot."

"A foot? What about the All-Is-Lost?"

"I hear it's creeping up a ways on account of being in the same neighborhood. I think it hit $10 a foot, but that can change at any moment."

"Where can I sell the claim?" Nathan asked.

"Just go down in front of one of the assay offices and start shouting. Someone's bound to make you a deal."

Nathan turned Onepenny around.

 Son, be sure and tell Push-Bill I'll buy his goods. And listen...if you rake in some cash on that deal, you better get out of town or hide that money. It ain't too safe around here at night."

Nathan nodded and rode back down toward the crowded street. He found a noisy shouting match in front of the Northern Nevada Assay Company. He dug out the stock certificate and waved it around shouting, "One hundred feet of the All-Is-Lost!"

After several unsuccessful attempts to attract attention, he rode Onepenny through the crowd and up onto the wooden sidewalk. Then he climbed up and stood on the saddle and shouted at the top of his voice, "One hundred feet in the All-Is-Lost!"

For a moment everyone stared at Nathan. Then in one instant everyone began to yell and scream.

"Get that horse off the sidewalk."

"Move it, kid."

"I'll give you $5 a foot."

"What?" Nathan dropped back down into the saddle and leaned over to a man wearing a tall silk hat. "How much?"

"$5 a foot."

"It's worth $10," Nathan shouted.

"Says who?" the man pressed.

"Me!"

"$5 is my last offer," the man called out.

Nathan felt someone tugging at his other leg. He leaned over to the opposite side of the saddle.

"Son, you still got the All-Is-Lost?"

"Yep."

"I'll give you $6 a foot."

Nathan sat back up and yelled down to the first man, "He'll give me $6."

"$7," the man shouted back.

Then the one on the left yelled, "$8. "

"He's a fool," the first man shouted.

Nathan was about ready to concede to the $8 price when the first man roared, "$10. I'll give you $10 a foot."

"It's a deal," Nathan shouted.

The man began to scribble something on a paper.

"I want cash, Mister," Nathan called.

"Cash? Well, I don't—"

"Cash, and now!"

"But that's not the way—"

Nathan pushed back his hat. "Cash!"

Mumbling in the roar of the crowd, the man dug out a poke of gold coins and counted out fifty coins.

Nathan handed the man the paper. He held it up for inspection. Then he handed the coins to

Nathan, who shoved them into his saddlebag and buckled it down.

Determined to make it out of town as soon as possible, Nathan spurred Onepenny down off the sidewalk and through the crowd. As he left, he heard the man who had bought the stock yell, "One hundred feet in the All-Is-Lost. Only $15 a foot."

He didn't look back. He hurried out of town and started back down the road. Most of the rigs and horses were still pulling into the hillside town, but a few, like Nathan, were leaving. He didn't think much about the people around him until he noticed two unshaven men riding about thirty feet behind him.

They're following me!

CHAPTER 7

Nathan didn't look back again, but when he crested a hill and calculated he was out of their sight for a moment, he pulled his carbine out of the scabbard and laid it across the pommel of the saddle.

Money fever is crazy. Everybody wants more and more until they begin to act without judgment. The only reason in the world for the existence of 10 is so that someone might get rich. It's like gambling...only instead of chips, you put your life on the line.

Lord, I can't face these men down like my father can...so you've just got to help me!

Several miles out of town the road dropped down into a dry creek bed where one lightning-struck cottonwood tried to survive. The limbs were dwarfed close to the broken trunk, and the leaves were turning prematurely yellow. Next to the tree was a parked stagecoach. Two men were making repairs to a rear wheel, and the passengers, all women, were sitting in what shade the tree offered.

He rode right up to the women and blurted out under his breath, "Ladies, I'm Nathan T. Riggins of Galena, and I think a couple of bushwhackers are following me. Could you pretend like you know me, and maybe they'll ride on by."

His eyes searched their faces for sympathetic eyes. In the background he could hear hoof- beats coming closer.

This is dumb. They have no idea what I'm talking about.

The dark-haired woman in the bright yellow dress stood up and called, "Why, Nathan, honey. How good it is to see you. Come on down and give Kay Lynn a hug."

He hardly hit the ground when the woman threw her arms around him and squeezed him blue. "How am I doin', kid?" she whispered.

All Nathan could do was nod.

"How's your mama and daddy doin' down in Galena? Or did they move to 10? If they're in 10, we'll have to have a party tonight. Girls, this is my good friend, Mr. Nathan T. Riggins."

Nathan peeked down at a girl who looked about eighteen or nineteen.

"They're gone, Kay Lynn. You can cut the play actin'." She shrugged.

Nathan glanced around and saw the men far on down the road to the south.

"Thanks, Miss...eh, Kay Lynn."

"Who were they?" she asked.

"I don't know, but they've been following me awful close for several miles."

She stared Nathan right in the eyes. "Why?"

"'Cause folks in 10 are gold crazy...and, well, they thought I might be carrying some color."

"Are you?" one of the other girls asked.

"Of course he is," Kay Lynn scolded. "Why else would a young man like this come riding straight up to us." She glanced over at the men working with the broken stagecoach. "Foshee, how long until we're on the road?"

A red-faced man glanced over at the women and grumbled, "I'm workin' as fast as I can. I told ya, I'll get you up to 10 before dark...now I'll do that if I have to carry you on my back."

"Well, Nathan," she continued, "I think we'll probably be here a while. Why don't you just stay with us a spell and give the men a chance to get on down the trail?"

She's got to have one of the best smiles I've ever seen...next to Leah's. "Yeah, I could use a little rest. I rode all last night," he managed to reply.

"Well, pull up some shade and take a nap," she invited him with a broad smile.

Nathan hitched Onepenny to the back of the parked stagecoach, jerked off the saddle and blanket, and carried the heavy saddlebags over to the shade. He noticed the women glancing at the saddlebags.

"Eh...just thought I'd use these for a pillow," he explained. "Your poke's safe with us, Nathan T. Riggins. At least," Kay Lynn grinned, "with most of us."

He could smell a strong perfume that reminded him of a rose garden. "Why are you going to 10? It's a lousy place for ladies...I mean, it's a lousy place for anyone."

"A man named McSwain hired us out of Denver to come and wait tables and serve food in his fine hotel," Kay Lynn replied. "McSwain? You mean the Colorado House?"

"Yes."

"Oh, no!"

"What's the matter? We hear it's the foremost hotel in 10."

"Eh...yeah, I guess you could say that." Nathan shrugged. "It's a busy place—that's certain...lots of hard work."

She nodded. "He promised us room and board and $65 a month. That sure beats teaching school."

Nathan laid back on his saddlebags and closed his eyes. Several of the women asked him other questions about 10. His answers came slowly as he drifted off to sleep, trying to imagine the excitement a coach load of pretty women would stir up in the town of 10.

◆ ◆ ◆ ◆ ◆

When he finally opened his eyes, the sun had disappeared in the western mountains, but plenty of daylight reflected off the blue summer sky. Miss Kay Lynn was shaking his shoulder. She held a lemon-colored parasol over her shoulder, and he noticed for the first time that she didn't have any lines drawn tight around her gray-green eyes, like his mother did.

"Nathan T. Riggins, we're pulling out. Did you want to ride back to 10 with us?"

Nathan propped himself up. "What? Oh...no. I need to go on down the trail. I've got to get this money...I mean, I've got to find Push-Bill." He flung the saddlebags over his shoulder, making sure he heard the coins rattle.

"Oh, they're still there." Kay Lynn smiled. "All fifty $20 gold pieces."

"How did you...?"

She lifted her light brown eyebrows. "Not all of us used to be schoolteachers."

◆ ◆ ◆ ◆ ◆

By the time Nathan saddled Onepenny, the stagecoach was a trail of dust to the north. With no one within sight, Nathan crammed papers from his saddlebags into his pockets and dropped twenty-five coins in each boot, pulling his trouser legs back over them. He could hardly walk with the added weight rattling around on each foot, but he scooted over to the dry creek bed and filled his saddlebags a third of the way full of pebbles. Then he awkwardly climbed aboard Onepenny and trotted back onto the road.

"If Push-Bill's made it to his usual camp, we should be coming across him about dark," he mumbled.

Nathan proceeded slowly, carrying his carbine in his lap. Every hill became a possible hiding place. Every big sage, a reminder of ambush. Every ravine, a threat. It was a good hour and a half later that he pulled up at the top of a steep downward grade.

If I was going to trap someone on this road, this would be the place. A couple of men could hide against that mountain on the left, then charge whoever's on the trail. Folks would naturally pull off to the right and make a run for those rocks, but that's the edge of a canyon. They could trap somebody over there and ...

"Wait," he blurted out to the horse. "If they're watching, I can't go to the left, and I can't slip by on the road unnoticed. Maybe we could ride

98

right along the edge of the canyon on purpose. No one would look over there."

The evening shadows were starting to fade when Nathan turned Onepenny off the trail and toward the edge of the canyon.

Nobody in his right mind would come out here on purpose...that's why it's a safe route.

Nathan rounded the boulders and slowly picked his way along the rocks, hoping to put a few of them between himself and the road. Constantly glancing over at the road and the hills beyond, he let Onepenny find his own way.

While he was still gazing over his shoulder, without warning a man jumped out in front of him, waving a revolver and screaming, "Don't lift that carbine, boy."

Nathan reacted by spurring Onepenny to the right and found himself trapped at the canyon's edge. Northern Nevada's great basin stretched out in front of him. He whipped the horse around to look for an escape and found himself facing two men on foot, with guns drawn.

"Don't raise it, boy, or you're dead," one shouted.

"Sure was nice of you to ride right up to us. We had given up on you and camped over here for the night."

"Yep," the other one agreed. "We thought for sure you rode back to 10 with that load of women. But you waltzing into camp like this makes a man believe in divine Providence, now don't it?"

"Now just toss us that saddlebag of coins, and we'll let you ride away," the other demanded.

Nathan didn't attempt to raise his gun. "It doesn't belong to me. I can't give it away."

"Well, now...if it don't belong to you, it sure ain't worth dyin' fer, is it?"

"I promised to deliver it to a friend," Nathan pleaded. "Well, you didn't promise to git yerself killed over it."

"If I give you the saddlebags, you'll let me go?"

"Sure 'nough, won't we, Janton? We ain't got no use for you."

"But I can't ride away. You got me blocked in."

Peering through the evening shadows, Nathan continued to search for a way out.

Lord, You promised never to leave me or forsake me. Well, where are You now?

One of the men waved his arm at the other, and both men scooted over to the north.

"Drop the saddlebags right where you sit and ride on out to the south."

Nathan slowly transferred the rifle to his left hand so he could more easily cock it if he needed to. "You won't shoot me in the back, will ya?"

The man impatiently shifted his weight and pointed his revolver at Nathan's head.

"I'm going to shoot right where you sit. Now throw down that gold."

Nathan reached back and lifted the rock-heavy saddlebags. At the same time that he held them out to the left of Onepenny, he shook his right boot to make it sound like the coins were in the saddlebags.

"Throw it down, boy. It's your choice."

"No," Nathan spoke slowly and softly. "It's your choice."

"What?"

100

"You can follow the saddlebags, or you can follow me," he shouted.

With that, he flung the heavy saddlebags over the edge of the canyon and spurred Onepenny. As he did, he swung around the horse's neck, which shielded him from the outlaws.

Two shots fired into the air, but Nathan was flying through the shadows within seconds. He turned onto the road at a full gallop and ran Onepenny for about fifteen minutes before giving him a rest.

Neither of them will want to leave the other with those saddlebags. They won't chase me until they find the pebbles.

It was a long, dark, cautious, menacing hour before Nathan recognized some wagons in the moonlight and noticed two familiar white mules on the picket line.

"Let's take it easy, boy. I don't want to startle Push-Bill and his scattergun."

As they sauntered a little closer, Nathan noticed the freighter had his shirt off and his hands up in the air, and Quickly had an armlock on him.

He's got Push-Bill!

Slipping off Onepenny, he scooted his coin-filled boots along behind the freight wagons, holding his Winchester in hand.

He heard bones crack.

"Wagh," Push-Bill screamed, "you like to killed me that time!"

Nathan dove under the wagon and rolled up on his feet, shoving the barrel of the carbine into Quickly's back.

"Turn him loose, or so help me, I'll pull this trigger," Nathan shouted.

"Whoa, boy, whoa," Quickly hollered releasing Push-Bill.

"Nate?" Push-Bill called. "Back off there, son. I was jist havin' Quickly straighten out a crick in my neck."

"What?"

"He was helpin' me...at least he was a tryin'," Push-Bill insisted.

"Oh," Nathan sighed, "I thought he was—"

"We know what you thought," Push-Bill interrupted. "We got worried about you bein' so late and all."

"I was bushwhacked."

"No! Did they hurt ya?"

"Nope."

"Did they get your goods?" Quickly pressed.

"Only a saddlebag full of rocks."

"Who was it?"

"One tall, one short. I think I heard the name Janton."

"Janton and Claymore! The two ol' boys that cheated me and lifted your poke."

Quickly stepped toward the fire. "Did you find Chance Aragon?"

"Yeah."

"Did he buy the certificate like I said?"

"Nope."

"No," Quickly gasped. "But he promised he would—"

"Aragon's not making any more deals. He's lying six feet under. But I sold the claim on the street."

"You did?" Push-Bill pulled on his shirt and walked over to Nathan. "How much did you get?"

102

Nathan pulled off his right boot and poured the contents into Push-Bill's hands.

"$500? You got $500?"

"Nope." Nathan hobbled over to Quickly. Then he pulled off his other boot and poured the contents in front of the man. "I got a thousand. This part is for Mr. Quickly."

Quickly jumped to his feet. "A thousand! Didn't I tell you it was a winner?"

Push-Bill and Quickly danced around the campfire. Finally, when they calmed down, Nathan told the whole story.

◆ ◆ ◆ ◆ ◆

At daylight Quickly saddled up while Nathan and Push-Bill hitched up the team. "Got to go down to that new silver strike in

Arizona before the rush," he called to them. "You was really goin' to hang me, weren't ya?"

"Yep," Push-Bill replied.

"Well, boy...keep that old man alive. His temper will bring him down one of these days." Quickly tipped his hat to Nathan and rode off to the south.

"Do you think those two will be waiting for us up on the trail?" Nathan asked.

"Nope. They sound like a couple of sneak thieves that don't do nothin' unless it's at night and they got good odds. Out on the trail in daylight will be all sorts of folks headin' up to 10. Besides, from what you described, they're probably still trying to find a way to get down the canyon to retrieve those saddlebags."

◆ ◆ ◆ ◆ ◆

The trip back into 10 with the freight wagons was uneventful. Nathan and Push-Bill left town the moment they unloaded. They camped that night not far from where they had the previous morning.

"We won't be staying in Galena for three days this time," Push-Bill announced. "We've got to get back up here while the prices are high."

"I need to go out to the Rialtos' and get my dog," Nathan mentioned.

"You take that shortcut the girls showed you tomorrow, and then meet me at Bobcat Springs," Push-Bill suggested. "Measure them narrow parts and see if a wagon might pull through. I ain't very thrilled about blazing trails with a freight wagon, but if I could save half a day, it might be worth the risk."

"Yes, sir."

"And don't be dallying around with them girls. It's time to make big money. I'll pay you double wages as long as this boom holds up."

Nathan pulled the mining claims out of his pockets, started to turn and pack them back in his saddlebags, and then remembered he didn't have any. Looking at each claim closely, he stuffed them one at a time back into his pockets.

"What you lookin' fer?" Push-Bill inquired.

"I was wondering if one of these was for the Antelope Flats Mine. It was selling for $500 a foot. Hey, look at this."

"You got one?"

"Eh...no, but I found twenty feet of the All-Is-Lost. I didn't know I had that. I could have sold it for $200. But maybe the price will go even higher.

104

If this one goes to $500 a foot, that would be...$10,000! I could buy a ranch with that."

"Well, don't go buyin' nothing on speculation. When we return to 10, you can sell all the scraps of paper you want."

It was a little before noon when they came to the cutoff, and Nathan rode down toward the western mountains. The trail seemed longer than before. He found himself wanting to hurry to the ranch.

Turning down the row of trees, he glanced behind every one trying to spot the girls. Finally, he saw some slightly dusty toes peeking out from one of the tree trunks.

"Is that you, Babe?" he called.

The six-year-old poked her head around the trunk. "I wanted you to see my toes." She grinned.

"Where are your sisters?" Nathan asked. "I expected to see them out here with a shotgun."

"They're busy with chores. So they sent me out. Sal said it was only that Nathan boy, so there was no reason for them to stop work."

"You want to ride with me?" Nathan asked.

"Yep," she giggled. "Can I ride on top those spots?"

Nathan pulled her up behind him and let her sit on Onepenny's rump, holding onto the cantle.

"How's Tona?" he asked.

"Nan says he's mostly dead, but Sal thinks he might pull through. He can't eat or walk, but Cape gets up in the night and makes sure he gets some broth."

Nathan rode silently for a while.

Lord, maybe I should have...I just couldn't, Lord. I mean, he's been...he's just too ...

"Hey, are you crying?" Babe blurted out.

Nathan wiped his eyes. "No...it's the dust. Just something in my eye."

Riding into the yard, he saw several of the girls ambling over to the front porch.

"Boy, your dog isn't going to make it," Nan announced. "Here, let me take your pony."

"He is too going to make it," Babe cried out as she slid down off the back of the spotted horse.

"I think he'll be o.k." Cape nodded as she brushed back her blonde hair. "But he's still feeling poorly."

Nathan crouched over Tona who was lying on some blankets in a large crate on the porch. The dog didn't even try to raise up. He didn't turn his head or move his eyes. But his tailed thumped several times against the wooden box.

"That-a-boy...you just rest." Nathan patted the back of the dog's neck and scratched his head. "You've got to pull through, Tona. I need you!"

Lord, he's dying, isn't he?

When Nathan looked up, Sal stood beside him. "He's doing a little better, but we can't get him to eat on his own."

"I've fed him every night since you left," Cape informed him. "I sure do appreciate it. You ladies looking after my dog. It's...*I am not going to cry*...it's one of the ..."

"Can you stay for supper?" Sal invited. "We would enjoy the company. Perhaps you could spend the night. There's plenty of room in the barn."

"I really need to take Tona and get back to Bobcat Springs.

We're in a hurry to get another load up to 10. Prices are going crazy, and it's a good time to sell freight."

"Well," Sal said thoughtfully, "maybe this would be a good time for us to ride up and sell the produce from the garden. But you can't move that dog. He's just living a day at a time, and there's no way he could make it back to Galena."

"But I can't ask you to...I mean, I just don't feel right having you take care of him."

"We don't mind, really," Beth insisted. "Tona has become kind of a project for us."

"Well...let me pay you something. It's really worth a lot to me and—"

"Nathan, that would be insulting to our hospitality," Sal insisted.

"But...listen," he protested. "Look, if you're going up to 10 ..." He jammed his hand into his pocket and pulled out a wad of crumpled papers. "Look, I got all these little mining claims for a sack of beef jerky. I know one of them's worth $250, but you take them all. Sell them in 10 and keep the money."

"How many do you have?" Cape asked.

"I think there's eight of them, but like I said, I don't know if any of them are worth anything except for that one."

"Which one is that?" Sal asked.

"The All-Is-Lost Mine," Nathan replied.

"Well, we couldn't—," Sal began.

"Please," Nathan persisted. "It would insult my sense of fairness if you didn't take something. I mean, I don't know how long Tona will have to stay here."

"I'd like to own a gold mine," Babe said giggling. "Then I can buy a doll and a red hat and a book with pictures."

Sal glanced around at the girls who waited with expectant faces. "Well...Nathan, if you will take back this All-Is-Lost claim, we'll divide up the others. Each one can have one."

"But...I don't think they're worth—"

"That's the reason we're taking them. It will be fun for us to speculate, and you can have a clear conscience about leaving Tona here."

"Well, I...," Nathan mumbled, "that's fine with me, but I don't think you know how much that dog means to me."

"The tear streaks across your cheeks have told us that." Sal smiled.

"Those aren't tears. He just got dust in his eyes," Babe explained.

◆ ◆ ◆ ◆ ◆

Nathan drank some fresh milk and ate six warm oatmeal cookies before he climbed on Onepenny and left the Rialto ranch. He rode past the lane, crossed the plain, and entered the hills, climbing up toward Bobcat Springs. But his mind was still on the Rialto sisters.

Lord, Mr. and Mrs. Rialto did an awful good job with the little time you gave them. I suppose you got a pretty nice setup in heaven for folks like that. Keep the girls safe, Lord...and help them not be too bothered looking after Tona.

"Tona," Nathan muttered aloud. Suddenly Onepenny pulled his head around as if looking for the gray and white dog.

"He's not here, boy." Nathan patted the horse and rode on up the hill. He remembered how lifeless Tona had looked.

Tona's fought lots of bigger animals. He's whipped dogs five times the size of that bobcat. It's just not fair for him to get so ripped up. Lord, why did You have to create bobcats so mean?

Nathan rode into the springs ahead of Push-Bill. He built a small fire, waiting for the wagons to arrive. It was near dark before he heard the shriek of the wheels and Push-Bill's shout.

After camp-making chores were finished, they settled in for supper.

"Well," Push-Bill mumbled through his plate of beans, "every day that dog lives gives him more time to heal up."

"You should have seen him. He looks awful," Nathan admitted.

"Well, you and him learned a big lesson. Don't never dance with a bobcat. Now you just got to trust the good Lord's timing. You don't get to keep any animal forever...not that dog...not even that spotted horse."

"Yes, but..." Nathan's voice trailed off. "I was kind of hoping Tona would stick around until he died of old age." Nathan put down his supper plate and picked up his carbine.

"I'm going down by the springs," he announced.

"With your gun?"

"Maybe I'll shoot a rabbit."

"You ain't goin' rabbit huntin'," Push-Bill said.

◆ ◆ ◆ ◆ ◆

The sky was black, and the moon was out. Nathan crouched by the brush at the side of the springs—five cartridges in the chamber, the lever cocked, and his finger tensed on the trigger. Just as he was about doze off, something moved near the springs.

Out of the brush stalked the bobcat. Nathan pulled back the hammer with his thumb, and at that tiny click the bobcat broke for cover.

Blam!
Blam!
Blam!
Blam!
Blam!

Nathan lowered his gun and shoved in more cartridges. He threw his carbine to his shoulder to fire again.

"Nate!"

He spun around to see Push-Bill standing behind him.

"Give it up, son. You cain't shoot what you cain't see."

"I'm going to kill that bobcat. I'm going to kill it for Tona." Nathan's voice tightened and tears welled up once again.

CHAPTER 8

Leah Walker was sitting on a bench in front of her father's barbershop when Nathan, aboard Onepenny, led the freight wagons back into Galena. He rode straight up to her, slid down off the spotted horse, and brushed the road dust off his shirt and trousers. She wore the new green dress and a matching ribbon in her hair.

"Hi, Nathan," she called.

"Are you waiting for someone?" He glanced inside the barbershop window and waved to Mr. Walker.

"Maybe I am, and maybe I ain't."

"Is that Kylie guy around?"

"No, he went home last week. You know'd that," she answered, shading her eyes from the afternoon sun.

Nathan cleared his throat. "Leah, I want to talk to you right now."

"What about?"

"Well...I been figuring...it's time you made up your mind."

She looked down at the wooden sidewalk. "About what?"

"About me or Kylie. Listen." Nathan cleared his throat and swallowed hard. He didn't want his voice to sound high and squeaky. "It's either me or him. You're my girlfriend or you're not. But if you

111

are, you can't go around sayin' that you're going to marry Kylie. Now that's all there is to it. You make up your mind."

Leah didn't answer.

"Well," Nathan urged, "who are you going to choose?"

She wrinkled the freckles on her nose and sighed deeply. "You come ridin' in here like some Saturday night cowboy and want me to have an answer just like that?"

"I don't have much time. We're leavin' at daylight. Leah, it's been grindin' on me every night."

"Ever' night? You been thinkin' about me ever' night?"

"Yeah, it nags at me like a chore that needs doing," he replied. "So...it's a chore to think about me?" she teased.

Nathan could feel his face flush. "No, that's not it. But it has been on my mind most all week."

"Well, then, I ought to have a week to think about it, too, Nathan T. Riggins."

"But it will be nine days before I come home again."

"I'll let you know when I'm good and ready." She stood up and spun around toward the stairs that led to her house. "I thank you kindly for your offer, and I shall consider it presently," she announced and then ran up the stairs.

◆ ◆ ◆ ◆ ◆

Nathan plunged into a hot bath, changed his clothes, and ate a supper of fried chicken and mashed potatoes with his parents as he tried to explain everything from Tona's run-in with the bobcat, to the Rialto sisters, to selling the mining claim in 10. However, he didn't mention the bushwhackers.

"And I've got to go help Push-Bill load tonight. We're pulling out at daylight. He says we've got to get back while the prices are high. Did I tell you he's payin' me double on this trip?"

When he finished his second piece of yellow cake, he cleared his plate, brought his mother an arm load of wood for the breakfast fire, and ran out the door. Rounding the corner of the Mercantile, he was surprised to find Push-Bill organizing two complete teams of mules and two wagons behind each team.

"Is somebody going with us?" Nathan asked.

"Son," Push-Bill called, "I got a big favor to ask. I got a deal on a second wagon and team. And you, yourself, know how crazy prices is in 10. Well, I want you to drive one team, and I'll take the other."

"Me? I don't know—"

"I've seen you with the mules, and I know you can do it. I'll lead the way on this new team, and you can bring mine up. Old Rosie can lead them by herself—you know that. Besides, they'll be tired and not apt to act up. Now what do you say?"

"But...but...what about greasing the axles and the extra mules and—"

"I've already hired a couple of kids to help out," Push-Bill announced.

"Kids? Who?"

"Friends of yours, they said. The banker's son agreed to ride along, and—"

"Colin? You hired Colin?"

"Yep. Is he a good worker?"

"Eh...well, he's a—"

"No mind. He'll be a good worker after nine days with us."

"Who else did you hire? Most of the older guys are working in the Shiloh."

"Well, now, you're right about that. The second helper was a stickler, but I worked it out while I was getting a haircut."

"A haircut? At Walker's? You don't mean ..."

"Yep. I hired a girl named Leah. She was rarin' to come along, and her daddy said it was all right as long as you were on the trip."

"But you can't—"

"I did."

"But she can't..."

"Cain't what? Don't tell me she ain't a good worker either."

"No...no, Leah will work hard. It's just—"

"Good, that's settled," Push-Bill announced. "Besides, I'll only need them for this one trip. I hired Fergusen to round up a couple of clerks to work late and load all four wagons. You and me need a little rest, and then we'll start hitchin' up about 5:00 a.m. Are you up to it?"

"Eh...yes sir, I'll be here."

◆ ◆ ◆ ◆ ◆

And he was.

Sleepy-eyed, tired bones, raspy voice, and all—Nathan was hitching up the wheel horses and mules at 5:00 a.m.

114

At 5:30 a.m. Leah showed up wearing a faded long gray dress and heavy leather work gloves.

"Mornin', Nathan."

"Mornin'."

"Ain't it exciting that Colin and me get to go? Say, since you'll be on the team, can I ride Onepenny? I mean, I can take my dad's old mare, but I was thinkin'..."

Nathan gaped at Leah. She didn't look anything like the barefoot Leah he had first met the previous summer.

"Did you decide an answer to that question I asked ya last night?" he probed.

"Not yet. Can I take your horse?"

"Sure."

"Really?"

"Yep. You go get him out of the livery, saddle him up, and meet us right here. We're leaving at 6:00 a.m. you know."

"I'll be back."

"Leah," Nathan called, "roust out Colin. He's supposed to be here by now."

At 5:45 a.m. Push-Bill had his team ready to roll. It was 5:50 when Nathan drove his rig up behind the other. Leah came riding up on Onepenny at 5:55 and announced that Colin was on his way.

At 5:59 Colin Maddison, Jr., (with two d's) arrived at the wagons wearing woolly chaps and riding a black gelding. He carried a biscuit in each hand.

Push-Bill dropped his pocket watch back into his vest and signaled them to roll out at exactly 6:00 a.m.

115

The heat off the high Nevada basin drifted straight up, leaving a trail of dust hundreds of feet in the sky behind the wagons.

There were no bubbling streams.

No cool breeze.

No shade.

Just yellow-brown dust that caked Nathan's clothes, face, eyes, nose, and tongue.

By 9:00 a.m. Colin had pulled off the woolly chaps, Leah had tossed on an old broad-brimmed hat she borrowed from Push-Bill, and Nathan was getting comfortable with his own team.

Most of the time Leah rode alongside Nathan, and Colin plodded along next to Push-Bill. Only the creaking of the wagon wheels broke the silence of the empty landscape.

By noon Nathan had caught Leah up on most of the events of the previous trip. He talked to her while keeping focused on the team, but out of the corner of his eye he noticed her gazing at him. He wanted to whip around and catch her staring.

But he didn't.

"Is it like this for the whole nine days?" she asked.

"Oh, it gets steep further up. And more crowded. Folks coming off the train take the stage route that joins up above the springs."

"Is it pretty at Bobcat Springs?"

"The water's clear and cold...and there's still a little green grass. That's about it."

"And there's a bobcat."

Nathan instantly reached down for his carbine and then realized he didn't need it. "Yeah, well, it won't be there much longer. I told you, I'm goin' to blow its head off."

116

"Nathan, why do you keep goin' on and on about that old cat. That must be the sixth time today you talked about killing it."

"When you see Tona, you'll understand."

"Are we going out to that Rialito rancho?"

"Rialto ranch," Nathan corrected. "I think Push-Bill might want to try the shortcut. Anyway, I'm going to kill that cat before we get to the ranch."

"You sound just like Colin with that coyote last fall."

"This is different, Leah. Tona's not your dog. You wouldn't understand."

"I'm tryin' to understand, Nathan T. Riggins. But you ain't helpin' much."

The rest of the day was routine as long as Nathan didn't mention Kylie Collins and Leah didn't speak about the bobcat. All four were worn out that evening, and they crawled into their bedrolls right after supper. Push-Bill didn't even light a pipe or tell a single stretcher.

The second day started out identical to the first. About midmorning Colin rode back to Nathan.

"Is this it? Is this all we do? Mile after mile after mile of boring sagebrush and desert?"

"This is it."

"For nine straight days? You got to be kidding," Colin groaned. "Maybe something exciting will happen up over that pass."

It didn't.

Their wagons squeaked into Bobcat Springs about sunset, and everyone enjoyed washing up in the cold water.

After supper Push-Bill began a series of "ol'Jim Bridger" stories about a country that had

117

petrified trees, petrified birds, a petrified sun, and petrified songs. Colin's eyes grew wide, his mouth dropped open, and he didn't move as he got caught up in the story.

"I'm going down by the springs," Nathan announced, grabbing his Winchester.

"I'm going with you," Leah called. "I ain't never seen a bobcat."

"I'll bring it back to you, and you can make mittens out of the pelt," Nathan offered.

"I'm cornin' anyway," she asserted.

It was humid by the springs, and the moisture felt better than the daily dirt. Nathan scooted onto a rock amid the brush where he could look out across the springs. Leah scrunched up beside him.

"We can't talk," he whispered. "They're real skittish. No movement and no sound."

After about a half-hour, Leah leaned her head on Nathan's shoulder. A few minutes later she was asleep.

Lord, I really like being around Leah. She's fun, and she listens when I talk, and she makes me want to do things right. I think she's a good friend for me.

If I'm honest, well, I like the way it feels when she holds my hand or grabs me around the waist when she's riding behind me. Or now with her head on my shoulder. It feels real good. Is there anything wrong with that?

In the shadows Nathan spotted an almost familiar movement.

Here he comes! I can't see him, but I know he's there.

118

Silently Nathan lifted the carbine to his shoulder. The trigger felt cold to his finger, the stock extra hard against his cheek. He closed his left eye and took sight with his right. Then slowly he lifted his thumb and pulled the hammer back through the first muffled click to the second click.

He spotted movement—silent, eerie, like a floating shadow. A nose, an ear, then a head appeared. Finally, Nathan could see the bobcat's complete silhouette. He squinted and lined the sights behind its ear.

Then he heard a soft, warm whisper against the same ear where he could feel Leah's warm breath.

"Nathan, no! 'Vengeance is Mine, saith the Lord.'"

He lowered the Winchester an inch and peered out over the sights. Slinking up next to the adult bobcat was another about one- third its size.

A baby? This is the mother? I thought this was the father. Is this the same one? Did Tona stumble onto a mother and her kitten?

Just the thought of Tona brought back visions of the emaciated dog struggling for breath at the Rialto ranch. He raised the gun back up as the two bobcats cautiously drank from the spring. Once again the soft breath in his ear.

"Please, Nathan...You don't need this."

He paused, with dead aim on the bobcat who alternated between licking her paws and licking her kitten. Finally, he laid the gun silently across his lap. Leah's head still snuggled on his shoulder.

For a long time they sat there. The bobcat cared for her kitten. Just as the cat turned away

119

from the spring, a shout pierced the quietness.
Nathan and Leah jumped to their feet.

"Hey, you two. Push-Bill says it's time to
come back."

The bobcat and kitten disappeared. Nathan
and Leah hiked back to the camp.

"Did you see a bobcat?" Colin asked.

"Yeah." Nathan motioned. "A mother and a
baby."

"I didn't hear any shootin'? Couldn't you get
off a shot?" Push-Bill asked.

"Oh, I could have...I guess I just sort of got
tired of hating bobcats. You know what I mean?"

"Yep." Push-Bill nodded. "I guess hate of any
type just eats away at a man's soul. You let it go
long enough, and you ain't got nothin' in there
worth savin'."

"Well, I guess Leah talked some sense into
me," Nathan admitted.

"Me? I didn't see no bobcat. I slept through
the whole thing."

"Slept?" Nathan hooted. "What about all
those words you whispered in my ear?"

"I told you I haven't made up my mind yet
between you and Kylie, so don't go puttin' no
words in my mouth," she insisted.

"But. . . you told me...the bobcat and her
kitten...you said—"

"A kitten? She brought a baby? Why didn't
you wake me up?"

"Wake you up? You were awake and talking
to me."

"Nathan, don't you go 'round makin' up
stretchers about me. I was asleep and you know it?
I'm going to bed."

120

"Come on, Leah...you leaned over and put your lips right to my ear and whispered—"

"I did what?" Leah exclaimed.

"You said not to do it because I didn't need it, and you quoted from the Bible about vengeance."

"Nathan T. Riggins, I ain't never whispered in no boy's ear, and if I ever do, it won't be no Bible verses?"

"Maybe you were talking in your sleep. Maybe...maybe—"

"Maybe you was the one dreamin'," she huffed and stormed toward the last wagon.

Nathan couldn't think of what to say next, so he pulled out his bedroll, yanked off his boots, and crawled under his blanket.

Nathan stared at the stars and listened to the crackle of the fire. In the background he could hear Push-Bill telling another "ol' Jim and me" story to Colin. Somewhere, way off to the west, he heard a coyote howl at the moon.

Lord, this is sort of...peculiar. I distinctively heard Leah speak. I felt her warm breath. I remember the sound of her voice. It was deep and confident, crystal clear, yet soft and light...it was ...

Lord, somebody spoke to me. You know I'm not making it up.

You know that's why I didn't pull the trigger...

Lord? Was that You? Did You...I mean, did You sort of...maybe speak...or maybe use Leah even though she was asleep?

Nathan was still awake when Colin tossed his bedroll down beside him. He was still staring at the stars when Push-Bill poured coffee on the fire and

121

trudged off to sleep near the animals. He was still awake when the moon was high enough to reflect off the canvas wagon tops, making them glow like white ashes in a pine fire.

He didn't toss and turn like usual, trying to find a comfortable spot on the ground. He felt rested without sleep. A quietness stilled his mind. He had a deep sense of everything being right.

Lord, I can't remember feeling this relaxed in a long, long time. I'm glad I didn't shoot that bobcat. It was just being what you created it to be. Tona...I really want Tona to live. He helps me, Lord. You know, he reminds me about loyalty and being a good friend and bravery. But I'll let You decide about that. I just wanted You to know I think I can take it now...no matter what You decide about him.

◆ ◆ ◆ ◆ ◆

Nathan had started the fire and boiled the coffee before Push- Bill finished tending the horses and mules.

"You rolled out early," Push-Bill rumbled.

"Yeah. I was all rested and ready to get going. Are we going to take the shortcut through the Rialto ranch?"

"Well, according to your measurement we might have eight to twelve inches to spare, so I guess we'll give her a try. The main road will be so crowded with wagons I won't be able to pass nobody from now on. Roust 'em out and hook up your team while I fry some breakfast. The quicker we get on the road the better."

No one said much as they broke camp, scraped down some breakfast, and hitched up the teams. In fact, Nathan hadn't said more than a dozen words by the time they stopped the wagons to rest the animals at the trailhead leading back to the Rialto ranch.

Leah greased the axles on Nathan's wagons and walked up to where he was checking the rigging on the lead mules.

"Nathan, did you really think I was talking to you last night at the springs?"

"It's okay, Leah. Maybe I just thought I heard you speak."

"You ain't mad at me, are ya?"

"Nope."

Nathan noticed two long hair braids, and her hat pushed back on her head. "Is that the Rialto ranch, over against them hills?"

"Yeah...it's further away than it looks, but we'll be there by noon."

"Who lives there?" she asked.

"Didn't I tell you about all the ..." He paused mid sentence.

"All about the what?" she pressed.

"All the, eh...trees they planted along the driveway and the big garden and the animals and the horse barn and the—"

"No, you didn't tell me nothin' about it. You told me that some lady that reminded you of Miss D'Imperio was lookin' after Tona."

"Yeah, well there is one other thing ..."

"What's that?"

"You'll see." Nathan nodded. "Let's roll 'em out."

123

"Nathan, you ain't goin' to embarrass me, are you?"

"No, it's more like a surprise." He grinned.

❖ ❖ ❖ ❖ ❖

During the long, hot, dusty ride to the Rialto ranch, all four pulled bandannas over their faces to block the dust. No one felt like talking.

Push-Bill stopped at the entrance of the long, tree-lined drive. He signaled Nathan to take the lead into the ranch. Leah rode up beside him.

"I see what you mean. These trees sure do look out of place. It's like one of them oasis."

Nathan pointed to the trees. "You're about to meet some of the children who live at the ranch."

"Where? I don't see nobody."

Nathan pulled his bandanna down around his neck, whistled, and then called, "Come on out."

Instantly, a small brown head peeked around one of the tree trunks.

"Hi, Babe," Nathan called. "Who's with you?" Blonde-haired Nina, carrying a shotgun, stepped out behind her. "Just me, Nathan. Are you taking the back road up to 10?"

"Yeah, do you mind if we noon it at the ranch?"

"No, I'll go tell Sal." Nina turned and began to run down the long driveway well ahead of the team. Babe skipped up to Nathan's wagons which continued to roll along.

"Nathan lets me ride on them spots," she announced. "Well," Leah said smiling, "that sounds like a good idea." She reached over and pulled the six-year-old up behind her on Onepenny. "Is your

124

name really Babe? Or does Nathan just call all pretty girls by that name?"

"My real name is Babylon Rialto, but everybody just calls me Babe. I'm the youngest, you know."

"How many are in your family?"

"There's seven of us," Babe replied.

"Well, that sure gives you lots of friends to play with."

"Yes, I know," Babe said.

By the time the wagons rolled into the yard, Babe had slipped down and run to her sisters on the front porch.

"All seven children are girls?" Leah asked in astonishment.

Nathan laughed. "I told you there was a surprise."

"Their mother and father must have their hands full." Nathan stopped smiling. "Their mother and father are dead."

"Both of them? You mean, they live here all by themselves?"

"Yep. Come on." He signaled. "Let me introduce you." Nathan and Leah scooted off their mounts and walked toward the waiting sisters.

"Leah, this is Sal, Beth, Nan, Cape, and Jerri, and you met Nina and Babe." They all smiled at Leah.

"And this is—"

"I'm Leah Walker," she announced abruptly. Then slipping her arm into Nathan's, she disclosed, "I'm Nathan's girlfriend."

"Wh-what?" Nathan stammered.

"I'm ready to decide," she said under her breath. "And I choose you."

CHAPTER 9

For the next hour the only stationary living thing at the Rialto ranch was Tona. After Nathan checked on his dog, Nan and Cape helped him and Push-Bill run the teams out to the corrals. Sal and Nina dashed to the kitchen to prepare dinner. Leah scampered off to help them, and Nathan saw her point at him, giggle something to Sal, and disappear into the house. Jerri and Cape latched onto Colin, who offered no protest as they enlisted his help to set up a big table in the front yard.

Beth saddled a horse and galloped toward a hilltop behind the ranch. And Babe bounced around the whole yard in delight as if it were Christmas.

Nathan and Leah finally met on the front porch at Tona's crate.

"He don't appear good," Leah admitted.

"Well, he did lift up his head once," Nathan informed her. "He lost a lot of blood. He just can't seem to get his strength back."

"He's got a good place to rest. I allows they all like caring for him."

Nathan glanced around at the Rialto sisters. "They're an incredible family, aren't they?"

"Sometimes I wished I had some sisters," Leah said softly. "And if I did, these would be good ones to have. How come their mama and daddy had to die, Nathan? It don't seem fair. I thought it was bad not having my mom around...but at least I got my daddy."

"I don't know, Leah...I guess we all have different trails to follow through life."

"Well, I ain't going to complain anymore."

A fierce ringing of a dinner bell interrupted them. Babe beat the iron triangle with great enthusiasm.

Beth had just returned from her ride, and she organized everyone around the table. When the ladies were seated, Nathan, Colin, and Push-Bill also sat down.

"Well," Sal announced, "we usually take turns saying grace. But I think we should yield to our guests. Perhaps Mr. Horn will do us the honor."

"What? Oh ...," Push-Bill stammered. "Miss, thank ya fer offering, but I get to trippin' over my words when I pray. Nathan there, he's the one to do it. Go ahead, son." There was a pleading sound in the freighter's usually commanding voice.

The girls reached out, and everyone held hands. Nathan grabbed onto Leah and Babe.

"Eh...well, Lord, bless this food and help us all to gain strength from it. And we thank You for our friends, the Rialtos. Keep them safe and healthy. In Jesus' name, amen."

The second he raised up his head, Babe blurted out, "If you don't want your bread pudding, I'll eat it."

It took a good while before anyone was ready for dessert. By the time the bread pudding was served, most everyone could only manage a small portion, even Babe. Only Colin loaded his plate.

127

"Miss Sal," Push-Bill began, "if they ever make this shortcut the main route, you ladies should open up a business and serve meals. Half the men in 10 would pay $2 apiece for food like this."

"And the other half would pay it if they had $2," Nathan amended.

Push-Bill banged the table. "Now ain't that the truth." One single, long, loud bark burst out of Tona. Nathan jumped to his feet.

"Tona's feeling better," Leah said.

"Someone's coming," Nathan said. "I know that bark." Without saying anything, most of the girls scampered away from the table toward the barn and the trees in the driveway.

"Is something wrong?" Colin asked, taking another helping of bread pudding. "You know, this stuff is really good, especially if you put the cherry preserves on top of it."

"We don't like taking chances," Sal explained. "I don't see anyone on the drive. They must be on the shortcut."

Nathan and Push-Bill rushed over to their wagons for their guns.

"I don't see nothin'," Leah confessed as they returned to the table.

"That's what worries me," Sal warned. "Friends ride up in plain sight."

"Tona could be wrong," Nathan declared, "him being so bad off and all."

She looked right at him. "Has he been wrong before?"

"Eh...no, not really."

"Then they must be watching us from somewhere out there," Sal instructed. "Leah, pick

128

up some dishes like you're cleaning the table and take them into the kitchen and stay there. Colin, keep eating. Maybe they'll think we don't know they're watching."

"Yes, ma'am...I mean, miss."

"Nathan, you and Push-Bill keep those guns under the table. Let's wait for them."

"Do you think it's Indians?" Colin gasped.

"I don't know," Push-Bill answered, "but I'd better mosey out back and stand guard at the barn. I cain't afford to let 'em steal the stock."

Just as Push-Bill left, Nathan noticed a column of dust on the cut-off road. "One rider coming in from the north. Don't look back," he advised. "He's coming right over the ridge. It's...it's Janton!"

"Who?" Colin gulped.

"One of the guys that tried to rob my poke. He'll recognize me for sure."

Sal stood and walked straight at the oncoming rider, causing him to stop before he came near the almost deserted dinner table. Nathan sat frozen, turning his face away from the rider. His hands clutched the Winchester under the table. He could hear every word.

"Hello, I'm Sal Rialto. Can we invite you in for dinner?"

No, don't do that. Tell him to leave!

The man's right hand rested on the handle of his holstered revolver. His eyes scanned the grounds.

"I need to talk to your pa," Janton growled.

"I'm afraid you'll have to speak to me," she said.

"Look, woman, I saw an old man go over toward those mules. Tell him to come out here."

One glance at Colin's eyes, and Nathan knew the man was staring at them.

"Oh, yes, he's a guest. He's not my father."

"Well, go get him and your father. I'm in a hurry, lady."

"Would you like something to eat while you wait?"

"Just go get 'em."

A shout and a gunshot rang out from the barn. Then the mules bolted across the corral. Nathan didn't have time to lift his gun.

"Janton! Looky here what I found. If it isn't the old freighter himself."

Nathan looked up to see the one named Claymore holding a gun on Push-Bill as they walked slowly back into the yard.

"Well, now...it's not every month that you get to rob the same man twice!" Janton crowed. He dismounted and drew his gun. Walking toward Push-Bill, he seemed to be overlooking those at the table. As he got closer, he twirled and pointed his revolver at Nathan's head.

"Drop the carbine on the ground, boy. And stand up real slow," he commanded. "We know who you are, and you ain't pullin' no tricks on us this time."

"Shoot him, Janton," the other man called.

Ignoring his partner, Janton nodded at the other place settings. "Now jist call the rest of them back out here. We saw all them girls scatter out like chicks."

"Well, if this is the way you're going to react to our hospitality," Sal replied, "we'll have to ask you to leave."

"Leave? Do you hear that, Claymore? She asked us to leave." The man holding a gun on Push-Bill spat tobacco juice on the ground and sneered. "When and if we leave, it will be with a pack train of them mules loaded with wares, our pokes stuffed with gold coins, and a couple of them girls tied to the back of our saddles."

Push-Bill rammed his elbow into the man's rib cage and grabbed for the gun. It discharged into the air. Claymore pulled back and slammed the barrel of the gun into the freighter's head. Push-Bill dropped to the dirt.

At the same time, Colin dove under the table, and Nathan grabbed his carbine. But before he could lift it, Janton punched his revolver into Nathan's back. "You want to be a hero? I planned on only having to kill the old man, but if you want to die, too, that's all right with me."

For some reason Nathan could never explain later, at that very moment he felt as relaxed and peaceful as he had the night before, looking up into the stars. It was almost like a different voice that came out of his mouth.

"There's worse things than dying with a friend," he said calmly.

Sal swept her arm back toward the buildings and spoke clearly in an unhurried voice, "You understand, Mr. Janton, that you will have to kill all of us. We will all survive, or none of us will. And being gunmen, I assume you are aware of the capability of shotguns? You girls stick those barrels out a little more, please," she called in a loud voice.

131

From all around the yard the purposeful rattle of guns could be heard. Nathan glanced around and counted seven guns pointed at the men.

Seven? That means even Leah and Babe are armed.

"You're bluffin'," Claymore called out. "They're bluffin', Janton. They can't use them guns."

"We were all ranch-born and raised. I assure you, we can and will use these weapons," Sal replied.

"Miss Sal," Nathan called out, "you give the signal, and we'll drop to the ground. There's no use us getting caught in the crossfire."

"I was thinking the same thing, Nathan. Oh, and, Mr. Janton, if you don't mind, please stand back away from the table a little more. I wouldn't want to get blood on the linen cloth."

"What?" Janton stormed.

"Girls," Sal called, "do be careful not to hit Nathan or Colin."

Hearty replies echoed from all over the yard.

"I got a bead on the one pointing his gun at Nathan."

"Should I aim for his belt buckle or his head?"

"You aim at his feet, and I'll shoot the head, Nan."

"Leave some for me. I want something to shoot at."

"Let's just get out of here," Claymore suggested, straining his neck to see where the voices were coming from.

"I ain't letting a pack of girls bluff me out of nothin'."

"We will see that you get proper burial and that your families are notified," Sal continued.

"Wait," Claymore called. "I'm leavin'. Janton can do what he wants, but I'll jist ride right on out."

"I'm afraid that's impossible, Mr. Claymore," Sal continued. "You see, you assaulted Push-Bill, and now you will have to stand trial in 10."

"Stand trial? They don't have no sheriff, no judge, no nothin'."

"I'm sure they have a miners' court—right, Nathan?"

"Yep," he replied. "'Course Push-Bill being a good friend of most everybody, they might be mighty tough on 'em."

"I ain't standin' trial nowhere," Janton insisted. "Claymore, you shoot the woman. I'll shoot this kid, and we'll break for the horses."

"I ain't shootin' no woman. Every man in Nevada would come gunnin' fer me if I did that. Besides, if we shoot them, we give the others a clear shot."

"Well," Sal added, "there is one other possibility."

"What's that?" Claymore called.

"Reparation."

"What?"

"Yeah," Nathan responded, "you could pay Push-Bill for damages, and then there would be nothing against you."

"Pay him?" Janton cried. "You're crazy...we're the ones holding the guns."

"What do you think is fair, Nathan?" Sal ignored the gunmen. "Well, I'd say two revolvers, two rifles, and plenty of ammunition would be a good start."

"Yes, but I thought maybe two pairs of boots should be added to that," Sal replied.

"Yep, you're right." Nathan nodded. "Now if you will just throw down your guns, we'll get you on your way."

"Look, you ain't gettin' nothin' from me," Janton growled. Sal nodded at Nathan, and the two of them dropped to the ground.

"Oh, blast it," Claymore called, throwing his gun down. "Don't shoot, girls. I'm unarmed."

Janton broke for the horses, but Nathan slammed the barrel of his carbine around, cracking into the fleeing man's shins. Janton rolled to the ground, screaming in pain.

"Nan," Sal called, "come put a gun on Claymore. The rest of you stay put."

Within moments they had retrieved the rifles and extra ammunition from the bushwhackers' saddles, picked up the revolvers, and pulled off the men's boots.

"You cain't take them. It's stealin'," Claymore complained bitterly as he mounted his horse barefoot.

"We'll pack them up to 10 and leave them with the miners' court," Nathan informed him. "If you have a complaint, just go up and tell them about it."

Janton glared over at Claymore. "You ain't tellin' nobody about this...ever!" he growled.

Sal handed Claymore a half-filled flour sack. "What's this?"

"You men will need some supper."

Nathan spied a trail of dust moving quickly toward them from the west. "It looks like we have some more company."

"Maybe it's some cowhands from the XL Ranch," Sal guessed. "We invited them over for dinner. Now you two better ride hard in the other direction. I'm afraid the XL boys won't be quite as generous as we were."

Janton and Claymore kicked their ponies and galloped south. As soon as they left, the girls poured out of their hiding places, and Sal tended to Push-Bill.

"Who is coming in?" Nathan asked Beth.

"It's Beth's beau, Emery," Babe blurted out. "He works at the XL, and Beth rode up on the hill this morning to signal him over."

"Signal him?" Nathan asked.

"With mirrors," Beth explained. "We have a little code, and when he sees it, he comes over. I expected him by dinner time, but he probably got caught with chores."

Leah came out to Nathan carrying a fireplace poker.

"What are you doing with that?" he asked.

"It's my gun." She smiled. "Babe was holding a pipe, but the rest had real guns. We bluffed 'em, didn't we?"

◆ ◆ ◆ ◆ ◆

In less than two hours the yard was cleared, the teams were hitched, and Push-Bill had recovered. Emery received introductions all around, and Tona wagged his tail every time he heard Nathan's voice.

135

Push-Bill Horn made one last check of the wagons and mounted his wheel horse. Most of the girls gathered on the front porch. Sal, Beth, and Emery walked out to the wagons.

"Mr. Horn," Sal began, "Emery agreed to watch the place for a few days just in case those men decide to return. The girls and I were wondering if you could give us all a lift to 10. We've got vegetables, preserves, and sewn goods to sell and some mining stock to check on."

The old freighter, sporting a linen bandage instead of a hat, flashed a broad smile. "It would be our privilege, ladies. How much time do you need to get ready?"

"About thirty minutes. Can you wait?" Beth asked.

"Wait? You bet we'll wait," Push-Bill roared. "That'll give me time to eat that bread puddin' that I missed earlier. Tie 'em up, Nate. We're goin' to sit a spell."

CHAPTER 10

All afternoon the freight wagons creaked along the cut-off route with Rialto girls hanging all over them. Sometimes they rode on the wagons, sometimes on the mules. Sometimes they walked along beside.

Babe spent most of the afternoon riding the other wheel horse next to Nathan. Sal and Beth chose Push-Bill's first wagon. But the rest changed places so often Nathan couldn't keep track of them.

The heat and the dust were just as bad as always, but in the happy confusion everything seemed more bearable. Hardly a moment passed that he couldn't hear laughter and giggles. Leah traded off, letting each of them ride Onepenny.

That night, quartered at Wild Horse Canyon, the girls took over encampment. They stretched a tarp between the four wagons and made that their cabin, banishing Push-Bill, Nathan, and Colin to the fire ring and the livestock. They prepared a meal from supplies left over from the noon dinner at the ranch. After supper they started singing, and it was a good two hours before any of them decided to stop.

Sal and Beth, as always, got the girls rounded up and headed for bed. For most of the evening, Leah had so blended in with the others it was as if she were an eighth Rialto girl.

Finally, with Push-Bill and Colin down with the mules, it was just Nathan, Leah, and Sal sitting at the fire.

"You two sure acted calm out there with those outlaws today," Leah remarked.

"Well, don't let it fool you," Sal replied. "I was pretty scared...only ..."

"Only what?" Leah pressed.

"Well, sometimes you just know what you have to do. Part of being scared is not knowing what you should do next," Sal offered. Then she turned to Nathan and looked him in the eyes. "Were you scared?"

"I prayed awful hard," he admitted. "But I've been more scared than I was today. I don't know why. It was just kind of peaceful."

"Peaceful?" Leah gasped. "You could have been shot to death right in that yard."

"Yeah, well..." Nathan stammered. "I don't really know how to explain it. But I just knew that I would have to stop them from hurting any of the girls. The way I figure, it was kind of like my assignment."

"Assignment from whom?" Leah pressed.

"From the Lord, I guess." Nathan shrugged. "I don't know. Do you know what I mean, Sal?"

"Yes, I believe that's how I felt, too. We made a pretty good team, didn't we?"

"We sure did, Miss Sal."

"Nathan's my boyfriend," Leah reminded her.

"Well, I'm glad because if you hadn't come into the picture, I think Cape and Nan were going to come to blows over him. We don't get too many visitors back at the ranch."

138

"Cape and Nan?" Nathan exclaimed. "They don't like me at all!"

"You'll have to excuse him, Miss Sal," Leah commented. "He don't know much about girls."

Sal smiled and poked at the fire with a long stick. "Well, now they are arguing over Colin."

"Colin?" Nathan choked.

"Yes. There seems to be some fascination with a bank owner's son.

Nathan stirred the fire for a long time after Sal and Leah wandered off to bed.

Lord, I've sure had lots of adventures since I moved to Nevada. Some of them have been pretty scary...and some pretty happy. And sometimes I've had both on the same day. I'm grateful You were there every time.

He stood above the fire watching the coals pop and sizzle as he poured the coffee over them. The smoke and steam boiled up around his head. Suddenly he felt sleepy.

Stretching out on top of his bedroll, he used his blanket for a pillow and started to count the stars.

He fell sound asleep somewhere between six and seven.

◆ ◆ ◆ ◆ ◆

The next morning they found the road up to 10 packed with prospectors and pilgrims, freighters and foreigners, grocers and gamblers. True to form, Push-Bill passed half the rigs on the road, and Nathan had to struggle to keep up. The girls were all riding on the mule teams as they pulled up the last grade with the town in view.

139

"Why's he in such a hurry?" Leah asked Nathan.

"Well, for Push-Bill, minutes mean money. If all the wagons arrive at the same time, prices will drop. And if the mines go bust, there will be no market at all."

Colin came riding back to Nathan and Leah to report. "Push- Bill said he wants to roll right through town up City Street to Jacob's. He wants to sell and unload first thing. He said the girls can hop down at the assay offices and see if anyone wants to buy their claims. Then we'll all meet up at the Colorado House for supper."

"The Colorado House?" Nathan moaned. "These girls can't eat there."

"That's what he said," Colin reported.

"I'll tell the girls," Leah offered.

In a few minutes she came riding back to Nathan.

"Sal said they would take their goods to sell also. There's a market next to one of the assay offices."

"Did you tell her about Push-Bill wanting to eat at the Colorado House?"

"Yeah. She said it was the best place in town to eat," Leah related.

The final climb into 10 was steep, and the teams were barely trudging as they entered the town.

"They're building sidewalks," Nathan called out to Leah. "Last week there wasn't a sidewalk in town."

"Looks like a school or something's being constructed, too," she reported.

"A school?" Nathan called.

140

"No, it's going to be a church," Leah shouted. "Look, there's the steeple."

"In 10? A church? That's unbelievable," Nathan gasped.

"You know, the streets are pretty smooth, too."

"It's all so different. What did they get, a mayor or something?" Nathan wondered.

The crowds at the assay offices were just as boisterous as ever, but Nathan noticed a marked improvement in the way the men dressed. Many now sported silk hats and ties, and several looked as if they had shaved and taken a bath recently.

The wagons ground to a halt as Push-Bill tried to part the crowd. Sal, Leah, and the others slid down and unloaded their produce and preserves. Leah handed Onepenny's reins to Nathan.

"Can you take him to the corral?" she asked.

Nathan nodded and dug into his pocket. "Listen, you take this claim and sell it for me. Last week it was worth $10 a share. Maybe it will be more now."

"You mean, I'll be holding $200?"

"Or more."

"I ain't never had that much money before."

Nathan teased. "Well, if you're going to hang around me, you'll have to get used to big money."

The girls stepped toward the new sidewalk, and the whole crowd of men drew back and gave them plenty of room.

Push-Bill, Colin, and Nathan rolled into Jacob's, and within a matter of minutes they were unloading the wagons. About an hour later the task was done. Nathan and Colin led all the animals into the corrals.

"What's the thing on this Colorado House?" Colin asked. "The old man says the food's great, and Leah said you didn't like the place."

Nathan closed the corral gate and walked back toward Jacob's. "Well, the food is good, but you have to fight a dozen hungry miners for every bite. It's kind of like a war."

"What do you mean, a war?"

"You'll see," Nathan assured him.

Both he and Colin were engulfed by the massive arms of Push-Bill Horn.

"Well, boys, let's go get some supper. I'm buying for ever'body. I sold my wares for double the price and the extra wagon and team for triple what I paid. I ain't takin' no chances. I sent my profit down to Galena by Wells-Fargo. Now let's go get us a fine supper at the Colorado House."

"Push-Bill, do you think that's the kind of place to take girls?"

"They don't get no better in 10," he bragged.

As they came closer to the Colorado House, Nathan was astounded. The crowd outside stood in an orderly fashion, waiting in what looked very much like a line. A wide wooden sidewalk now graced the front of the restaurant, and several men in white shirts and ties sold dinner tokens.

"Looks like McSwain upgraded things a tad." Push-Bill elbowed Nathan.

"I don't believe this. Why would he change?" Nathan peeked through the window at the tables all set and waiting. "Tablecloths? They have tablecloths?"

142

"It's them women that's ruined the place," a big voice boomed behind him.

Nathan turned to see one of the hefty miners he had squeezed in next to on a previous trip.

"Women?" Nathan asked.

"Yep. Ever since McSwain brought in them serving girls from Denver, the place has started to be respectable. If this keeps up, 10 won't be a fit place to live." Then the big man paused, and his brushy beard parted into a wide smile. "But them gals sure is purdy...mighty purdy."

Nathan walked up to Leah and the others.

"This place looks all right," she announced.

"Yeah...well, it's changed. Trust me. Could you ladies sell any of those claims?"

"Yes," Babe shouted. "And we sold our produce, and we bought some things. I got my very own feather duster. Sal says I'm old enough to dust. And I got some candy and a book with pictures."

"You know," Leah added, "they offered Sal triple the usual price for the produce, but she wouldn't take it all. She said it wasn't right for anyone to have to pay that much for food."

"Did you sell my...it's our turn already? Now remember, grab all the food you can because...what's this?"

"I guess they seat you at a table now," Push-Bill mumbled. "Ain't this somethin'?"

The whole party of eleven stepped into the restaurant, and a uniformed serving girl showed them where to sit.

"Say, aren't you that Nathan boy?" she asked.

"Yes, ma'am."

143

"Well, we met down at that draw when the stage needed repairs."

"You ladies really changed this place," Nathan added.

"Oh, my yes, you wouldn't believe how horrid it used to be." Nathan turned to Leah. "See? I told you it used to be awful." When everyone was seated, the waitress began to bring them their food. As they settled down with meat and potatoes, Nathan suddenly sat straight up.

"The claims! I forgot about the claims. Could you sell any of them? Leah, what did you get for my claim?"

Leah glanced over at Sal, then back at Nathan, and then back at Sal.

"Eh...we'll give our report first," Sal offered. "I had seventeen feet of the Lucky Seven, and I got $9.10. I spent it all on yardage."

Beth was next to speak. "Well, thanks to Nathan, I had twenty-two feet in the Alligator, and I received $22, which I already spent on primers and new slates for the children."

Then it was Nan's turn. "Mine was the twelve feet of the Pretty Nugget, and it brought $8.

Blonde-haired Cape spoke next. "This guy offered me $3 a foot for my Root-Hog-Or-Die footage, but I told him that none other than Nathan T. Riggins of Galena, Nevada, had told me it was worth $10 a foot and so—"

"No, that wasn't the one worth $10 a foot," Nathan corrected her.

"Well, anyway, I made the man give me $10 a foot."

"How many feet did you have?" Nathan asked.

144

"Six. Now I've got three gold coins that are all mine, and I'm never ever going to spend them...until I get married, of course." Jerri stood as if to give a formal speech. Her black braids bounced as she spoke. "I had twenty-one feet of a worthless hole in the ground, but a man got to feeling sorry for me and offered me $5, so I took it and bought some new shoes. Now I'm as tall as Cape."

"You are not!"

"Am too!"

"It's my turn," Nina called out. "I had twelve feet in the Broken Nose, and they gave me $6. I gave half of it to the church building fund, and with the rest I bought stick candy."

"What kind of candy? What store sells candy?" Colin chimed in.

"Well," Babe announced, "I had six feet of some old mine, and this man with a tall hat said I reminded him of his daughter and he gave me $6."

"And," Sal offered, "we all want to thank Nathan for his generosity. "

"That's great," he replied. "I didn't know those were worth anything at all. How about you, Leah? What was my claim worth?"

"Eh...well, you said it should bring $10 a foot, right?"

"Yeah, what did you get?"

"That was the price last week, right?" she asked.

"Yeah, right. Now what did you—"

"Well, something happened over the weekend at the mine."

"What?" Nathan spoke rapidly. "Did the price go up like the Antelope Flats?"

145

"Eh, no," Leah replied. "They broke into an underground stream, and the mine filled with water. They've abandoned it. Now the certificate is worthless."

"Worthless? You mean, nothing?"

"Zero."

"They can't do that. I sold some last week for $10 a foot."

"I'm sorry, Nathan," Sal replied, "but Leah's right. Look, if you need these other claims back, we can—"

"No, no, no." Nathan sighed. "They're yours. It's just...just..."

"It's a crazy business, ain't it, boy? Welcome to the mines." Push-Bill joined in. "Mr. Maddison with two d's, would you pass that cherry pie?"

All of a sudden a smile broke across Nathan's face, and he started to laugh.

"You ain't mad at me then?" Leah frowned.

"No." He grinned. "I was just thinking about that mine. It proved to be true to its name. I should have known better than to hang onto something called the All-Is-Lost."

"Nathan," a feminine voice shouted from across the room.

One of the serving girls threw her arms around him and hugged him. He recognized the strong perfume.

"Honey, why didn't you come look me up when you came to town?" she teased.

"Eh, Kay Lynn," he stammered, caught up in her flashy eyes. *She just might be the most beautiful woman in the whole world!*

"Me and Nathan were almost family," she said with a laugh.

"Listen," he hurried to explain, "this is the lady that helped me when the bushwhackers followed me. Kay Lynn, this is Push-Bill Horn, Colin Maddison, Jr. (with two d's), the Rialto sisters—Sal, Beth, Nan, Cape, Jerri, Nina, and Babe...and this is Leah Walker."

Leah stood up, placed one hand on her hip, tilted her head, and spoke with authority. "I'm Nathan's girlfriend, and I can tell you right now, he ain't never goin' to marry nobody but me!"

~~THE END~~

ABOUT THE AUTHOR:

STEPHEN BLY (1944-2011) published over 100 fiction and nonfiction books for adults and kids. He won the Christy Award for the Westerns category. His widow Janet and their three sons finished his last novel for him, Stuart Brannon's Final Shot, Book 7 in the Stuart Brannon Series. Find out more about this family project at the Bly Books website blog: www.blybooks.com/

Ask for a list of Stephen Bly books here: Bly Books, P.O. Box 157, Winchester, Idaho 83555

If you liked this story, tell a friend or family member. Or write about it for a school report or at your favorite online place...

OTHER BOOKS BY STEPHEN BLY
YOU MIGHT ENJOY:

The Stuart Brannon Western Series
Hard Winter at Broken Arrow Crossing
False Claims at the Little Stephen Mine
Last Hanging at Paradise Meadow
Standoff at Sunrise Creek
Final Justice at Adobe Wells
Son of an Arizona Legend
Stuart Brannon's Final Shot

Adventures on the American Frontier
Daring Rescue at Sonora Pass
Dangerous Ride Across Humboldt Flats
Mysterious Robbery on the Utah Plains

The Lewis & Clark Squad Series
Intrigue at the Rafter B Ranch
The Secret of the Old Rifle
Treachery at the River Canyon
Revenge at Eagle Island
Danger at Deception Pass
Hazards of a Half-Court Press

Retta Barre's Oregon Trail Series
The Lost Wagon Train
The Buffalo's Last Stand
The Plain Prairie Princess

49418302R00085

Made in the USA
San Bernardino, CA
24 May 2017